THE RIVER'S CHILDREN

RUTH MCENERY STUART

THE RIVER'S CHILDREN

PART FIRST

The Mississippi was flaunting itself in the face of opposition along its southern banks. It had carried much before it in its downward path ere it reached New Orleans. A plantation here, a low-lying settlement there, a cotton-field in bloom under its brim, had challenged its waters and been taken in, and there was desolation in its wake.

In certain weak places above and below the city, gangs of men—negroes mostly—worked day and night, reinforcing suspicious danger-points with pickax and spade. At one place an imminent crevasse threatened life and property to such a degree that the workers were conscripted and held to their posts by promises of high wages, abetted by periodical passage along the line of a bucket and gourd dipper.

"Gangs of men, reinforcing suspicious danger points with pickax and spade"

There was apparently nothing worse than mirth and song in the bucket. Concocted to appeal to the festive instinct of the dark laborers as much as to steady their hands and sustain courage, it was colored a fine pink and floated ice lumps and bits of lemon when served. Yet there was a quality in it which warmed as it went, and spurred pickax and spade to do their best—spurred their wielders often to jest and song, too, for there was scarcely a secure place even along the brimming bank where one might not, by listening, catch the sound of laughter or of rhythmic voices:

> "Sing, nigger, sing! Sing yo' hymn!
> De river, she's a-boomin'—she's a-comin che-bim!
> Swim, nigger, swim!
> "Sing, nigger, sing! Sing yo' rhyme!
> De waters is a-floodin'—dey's a-roarin' on time!
> Climb, squirrel, climb!"

At this particular danger-spot just below the city, a number of cotton-bales, contributed by planters whose fortunes were at stake, were placed in line against a threatening break as primary support, staked securely down and chained together.

Over these were cast everything available, to raise their height. It was said that even barrels of sugar and molasses were used, and shiploads of pig-iron, with sections of street railways ripped from their ties. Then barrels of boiling tar, tarpaulins, and more chains. And then—

And then there were prayers—and messages to the priests up at the old St. Louis Cathedral, where many of the wives were kneeling—and reckless gifts of money to the poor.

A few of the men who had not entered church for years were seen to cross themselves covertly; and one, a convivial creole of a rather racy reputation, was even observed, through the sudden turn of a lantern one night, to take from his pocket a miniature statue of St. Joseph, and to hold it between his eyes and the sky while he, too, crossed himself. And the boon companion who smiled at the sight did himself make upon his own breast a tiny sign of the cross in the dark, even as he moved toward his friend to chaff him. And when, in turning, he dimly descried the outline of a distant spire surmounted by a cross against the stars, he did reverently lift his hat.

"It can't do any harm, anyhow," he apologized to himself; but when he had reached his friend, he remarked dryly:

"You don't mean to tell me, Felix, dat you pray to St. Joseph yet, you old sinner! Excuse me, but dose passing lantern, dey give you away."

"Pray to St. Joseph? I would pray to de devil to-night, me, Adolphe, if I believed he would drive de river down."

"Sh! Don't make comparison between St. Joseph an' de devil, Felix. Not to-night, anyhow."

"I di'n' done dat, Adolphe. No! Pas du tout. Not at all. H'only, I say, me, I would pray to de devil if he could help us out."

He laughed and shrugged his shoulders as he added recklessly:

3

"Yas, I would be one mud-catfish caught on his forked tail—just for to-night—an' let him drag me behind him in de river, if—"

"But you mus' ricollec', de devil he don't play wid water, Felix. Fire is his—fire an' brimstone—"

"Ah-h-h! Bah, Adolphe! Who is trying to talk sense to-night? Dose row of warehouse yonder, dey are all full, an' on my one pair shoulder. My li'l' crop is nothing. I got in doze warehouse, waiting for a sure rise in de market—all on my obstinate judgment—Everything of my brudder, my t'ree cousin, my wife, my mud'-in-law,—just t'ink!—not to speak about t'irty-five or forty small consignment. Sure! I would pray to anyt'ing to-night—to save dem. I would pray to one crawfish not to work dis way. Dem crawfish hole is de devil.

"But dat St. Joseph in my pocket! My mudder, I am sure she put it dere. She an' my sisters, dey will all kneel many hours at deir prie-dieux to-night—po' t'ings!"

"An' yo' wife—she also, of co'se—"

"My wife?" The man chuckled. "Pff! Ah, no! She is at de opera. She knows I am watching de river. She believe it cannot run over so long I watch it. I married her yo'ng. Dat's de bes' way.

"Mais, tell de trut', Adolphe, I am going to church, me, after dis. Dere's nothing, after all, like God to stand in wid you! You hear me, I tell you to-night de rizzen our women keep good an' happy—it is faith. You know da's true."

"Yas, I believe you, Felix. An' me, I t'ink I will go, too. Any'ow, I'll show up at Easter communion. An' dat's a soon promise, too. T'ree week las' Sunday it will be here.

"All my yard is w'ite wid dem Easter lilies already. Dis soon spring compel dem. Wen you smell doze Bermudas above de roses in your garden in de middle of Lent, look out for Old Lady Mississippi. She is getting ready to spread her flounces over yo' fields—"

"Yas, an' to dance on yo' family graves. You may say what you like, Adolphe—de ruling lady of dis low valley country, it is not de Carnival Queen; it is not de

4

first lady at de Governor's Mansion. It is—let us raise our hats—it is Old Lady Mississippi! She is de ruling lady of de Gulf country—old mais forever yo'ng.

"In my religion I have no superstition. I swallow it whole—even when I mus' shut my nose—I mean hol' my eyes. What is de matter wid me? I cannot talk straight to-night. Mais to speak of de river, I mus' confess to you dat even when it is midsummer an' she masquerade like common dirty waters, I propitiate her.

"Once, I can tell you, I was rowing one skiff across by de red church, an' suddenly—for why I di' n' see immediately—mais out of de still water, mixed into bubbles only by my oars, over my hand came one big wave. I looked quick, but I could see only de sun to blind my eyes. Mais you know what I did?

"Dat bright sun, it reflect a small stone in my ring, one diamond, an' quick I slip it off an' drop it. It was de river's petition, an' what is a sixty-five-dollar diamond to a man when—"

"Dey ain' got no insanity in yo' family, I don't t'ink, Felix? Otherwise—excuse me—I would be oneasy for you."

Adolphe was smiling, and he mischievously lifted one brow and drew up his lips as if to whistle.

Felix smiled, too, as he replied:

"You needn't fear for me, Adolphe. Mais strong-headed ancestors, dey are nothing. Me, I could start a crazy line just as well as my great-gran'fodder. Everything mus' begin somewhere."

But he added more seriously:

"Non, I would do it again—if I was on such a trip. I tell you what time it was; it was—"

He dropped his voice and looked over his shoulder.

"You want to know what, precisely, I was doing at de moment de river demand my ring? I was praying to her! Sure!" (This last in a whisper.)

"Oh-h-h!" Adolphe's face lit. "Yas, I understand. I ricollec'. You mean about five year pas'—dat time yo' sister los' 'er firs' 'usband, when—?"

"Yas, exac'ly. So you see dat predicament in w'ich I was placed wid de river. I never liked po' Jacques Renault—" He shrugged his shoulders. "I never profess to like him, mais he was my brud'-in-law; an' my po' sister—you know Felicité—she is my twin. She done nothing but cry, cry, cry for fo' days an' nights, an' pay all 'er money in de poor-box to find him. An' dey tried every way to bring him up. So me, I say nothing, mais when de fif day is come I loan from my cousin Achilles his wide skiff, an' I start out, an' I row two mile below w'ere dey foun' 'is clo'es an' hat, an' den I pull up again—an' wid every stroke I pray to de river to grant me dat satisfaction to find po' Jacques an' to lay him in his grave.

"Tell you de trut', maybe I am a sinner to say it, mais I was half afraid in my heart dat maybe Jacques was playing 'possum an' some day he would come back; an' when somebody is dead—dat's one terrible dread, yas—to get such a surprise, especially for one widow, you understand. It is a restriction, more or less, according to—Well, never mind.

"You may b'lief me or not, mais when de river she require of me dat ring, laying her wet hand over my hand like to take it, at de same time she turn it to de sun—well, I am not stupid. I dropped it quick to her, an' den I looked close, yas, on de water, an' immediately I see one—"

"You said jus' now you saw only de glare of de sun—"

"Exac'ly—an' den, naturally, one black spot befo' my eye, an' I t'ink it is de sun; mais—

"Well, 't is a disagreeable picture. Never mind! De river she give me de swap, an' we had one fine funeral de nex' day; an' my po' sister Felicité had her consolation.

"So, like I say, what consideration was one small diamond ring for such a pleasure?

"A widow widout a grave is like a wind in Feb'uary—crying always forever aroun' de house, wid nowhere to go, an' in her eyes are all kinds of weather. Bff!

6

"It is great consolation, a grave. It is a half-way station between de home an' de church; an' a widow she need dat—for a w'ile.

"Tell you de trut', when I take time to t'ink, Adolphe, sometimes I am ashame'. So long I am prosperous I am all for dis worl'; den, when somet'ing come, like now, an' t'row me on my knees, I feel cheap befo' God, yas. Mais, wid de river so, what can a man do if he cannot pray? So, after to-night's experience, I am at home wid my li'l' family by eleven o'clock every night, sure."

"'Ow much chillen you got now, Felix? You go too fas' for my 'rit'metic."

"Oh, no, not too fas'—just fas' enough. Only nine in over ten year—mos' eleven year. Only six, by right. I engage for six; mais what can a man do when his lady present him wid one extra, once in a w'ile! I am de las' one to make remark on her for dat, too, biccause I come dat way myself—following behind Felicité. Twins, dey run in some families; an' you know now I am coming to like dem. Dey are so sociable, twins."

"Ah, my friend, you have plenty occasion to be one good man."

"Occasion! I am blessed. T'ink all I have got to be t'ankful! I got my mudder, my mud'-in-law, my fad'-in-law—all riligious people an' good—an' nine li'tl' one, like six stair-steps wid t'ree landings for de accommodation of de twins." He chuckled. "Yas, an' I am going to be good. No more dem soubrette supper for me. An' dem danse de—

"Mais wait! What is dat?"

A bell had rung, and a voice was calling out the depth of the water as shown upon a graduated scale marked low down against the pier. The announcement was half-hourly now.

"What he say? T'irteen inches an' a—Dat's a half-inch fall. T'ank God! Maybe St. Joseph an' our women dey save us yet, Adolphe."

"Yas, maybe. Mais I t'ink de winter is full broke in Minnesota, too. No more dat confoun' ice to melt. I looked sure for de water to fall down yesterday. Any'ow, one half-inch is hope. Here, take one cigar. I can smoke, me, on dat half-inch. You got any matches, Felix?"

In finding his match-box Felix's fingers came in contact with the tiny statue of St. Joseph in his pocket, but he was only half sensible of the fact in his nervous joy over the slight decline in the river.

"Hello! Here is Harold Le Duc!" he exclaimed, as, by the light of his match, he chanced to catch the presentment of a distant face in the darkness.

"Hello! Come along, Harry, an' smoke one cigar. We mus' celebrate dat insinuation dat de river is falling. Less dan one inch, it does not count, except to prove she is hesitating; an' you know de ol' saying, 'She who hesitate'— 'Hello, young man! You are good for sore eyes!"

The person addressed had come forward with extended hand.

When another match, lighting Adolphe's cigar, revealed the young man's face again, there was something so startling in its wonderful solemnity and beauty that both men were impressed.

"You won't smoke? An'why? Come! It is one great comfort, a li'l' smoke. Here, let me—"

He presented the cigars again.

"Well, I thank you, but excuse me now." Young Le Duc took a cigar with a smile. "I'll enjoy it later, maybe; but not until we see a little further. As you say, a half-inch is only a hint, but it is a good one. I am going now up the coast, where trouble waits, and I may need a steady hand before morning. But I think the worst is over. Good night—and thank you. The folks—they are all well?"

"Fine, all fine, and asking always for why you don't come to see dem."

But he had gone.

The eyes of both men followed the retreating figure in silence.

It was Adolphe who spoke at last.

8

"Ah-h-h!" he sighed. "An' yet we complain sometimes, you an' me, eh? I am t'irty-seven years old an' I got t'irteen healt'y chillen an' two gran'chillen, an' my wife—look at her, yo'nger an' happier wid every one—

"Oh, I wonder, me, sometimes, dat God don't just snatch Everything away jus' for spite, when we always complain so.

"Did you take occasion to notice dat w'ite hair against dat yo'ng face? An' dey say he never mention his trouble."

"I tell you, like we said, Adolphe, dat river she is—she is—"

He threw up his right palm, as if in despair of adequate language.

"T'ink of coming home from de war, already robbed, to find all gone—home, wife, child, family, servants, all obliterate', an' only de river's mark, green mold an' mildew, on de walls above de mantel in de house; an' outside her still face under de sky to answer, an' she heed no questions. She is called de father of waters? In a sense, yas, maybe. Mais, no. She is, I tell you, de mother of trouble—an' pleasure, too.

"She is, after all, de queen of dis valley, an' no mistake—dat river. When she need fresh ermine for her robe, she throw it over our cotton fields—"

"Yas, an' de black spots, dey are our sorrows. Dat's not a bad resemblance, no."

The speaker looked at his watch.

"Pas' eleven," he said. "Da' 's good luck when she start to fall befo' midnight. Oh-h-h! Mais she is one great coquette, yas. She keep you crazy until she get tired wid you, an' den she slip away an' steal her beauty-sleep befo' de clock strike twelve."

"You t'ink she is going to sleep now? Maybe she fool us yet, Adolphe."

"Well, maybe. Mais I have great hope. She begin to nod, and when dat happen to a woman or a riv—"

Conversation was suddenly interrupted here by a great crash. The two men started, and, turning, saw an entire section of the improvised embankment fall landward.

Had the stress of the moment been less, they would involuntarily have hastened to the spot, but terror fixed them where they stood. There was but a moment of suspense,—of almost despair,—but it seemed an eternity, before relief came in a great shout which sent vibrations of joy far along the bank, even to those who watched and worked on the right bank of the stream.

It had been only a "dry break." The weights thrown in upon the cotton had been out of plumb, and had pitched the whole structure inward.

The uproar following this accident was long and loud, and had not subsided when the bell rang again, and, with tense nerves strained to listen, the line of men dropped speech. Instead of calling out the decreasing depth, as usual, the crier this time shouted:

"Two inches down, thank God!"

Screams of joy, not unmixed with tears, greeted this announcement. The strain was virtually over.

The two rich men who had stood and talked together mopped their foreheads and shook hands in silence.

Finally it was the older, whom we have called Adolphe,—which was not his name any more than was his companion's Felix,—finally, then, Adolphe remarked quite calmly, as he looked at his watch:

"I am glad dat cotton in de pile is saved, yas. 'T is not de first time de ol' city has fought a battle wid cotton-bales to help, eh, Felix? All doze foundation bales dey belong to Harold Le Duc. He contribute dem, an' make no condition. All dat trash on top de cotton, it catch de tar; so to-morrow we dig it out clean an' give it to him again—an'—an'—

"Well—"

He looked at his watch again, keeping his eyes upon it for a moment before he ventured, in a lower tone:

"Well, I say, Felix, my boy, what you say?"

"I di'n' spoke. What you say yourself, Adolphe?"

"'Well,'—dat's all I said; jus' 'well.' Mais I di'n' finish. I begin to say, I—Well, I was just t'inking. You know to-night it is de las' opera—don't you forget. No danger to make a habit on a las' night; ain't dat true? For why you don't say somet'ing?"

"Ah-h-h! Talk, ol' man! I am listening." Felix looked at his watch now. "An' maybe I am t'inking a li'l' bit, too. Mais go on."

"Well, I am t'inking of doze strange ladies. I am sure dey had many vacant box to-night. Don't you t'ink dey need a little encouragement—not to leave New Orleans wid dat impression of neglect? We don't want to place a stigma upon de gay ol' town. My carriage is here, an' it is yet time. One hour, an' we will forget all dis trouble. I need me some champagne myself."

Felix chuckled and shrugged his shoulders.

"Ah-h-h! Yi! An' me, too, Adolphe. I tol' you I was t'inking also. Mais let us sen' de good news home, an' let doze women off deir knees an' go to bed. My mud'-in-law she is de devil for prayin', an' she is poody stout, po' t'ing!

"We telegram it. Tell dem deir prayers are answered—de water is down—"

"An' our spirits are up, eh? An' we will be home in de morning, when de valuable débris is removed."

Felix laughed and touched his friend in the ribs.

"You are one devil, Adolphe. Mais we mus' be good to our women."

"Sure! I am going to return dat compliment you paid me jus' now. You say I am one devil, eh? Bien! An' in response, I say, Felix, you are one saint. You hear me! I say, one saint—uncanonized! Any man dat will telegram a message to save his rich mud'-in-law from maybe sudden apoplexy, he is one saint, sure! Mais you are right. We mus' be good to our women. A happy wife is a joy forever!"

11

He laughed again as he added:

"Mais de débris! Yi, yi! Dat make me smile. You ricollec' de las' débris, when Ma'm'selle Koko—"

"Ah, yes, Felix! Sure, I remember. I paid, me, I know, one good round sum for my share. Dat was one terrible smash-up. Two dozen champagne-glass; one crystal decanter; one chandelier, also crystal, every light on it broke, so we had to put off de gas; an'—well, de devil knows what else.

"Tell de trut', I don't like dat dancing on de supper-table, Felix. 'T is superfluous. De floor is good enough. An' you know, when a lady is dancing on a table, after a good supper, of co'se every glass is a temptation to her slipper. An' slippers an' wine-glasses—well, to say de least, de combination it is disastrous.

"So, I say, de floor it is good enough for me. It seem more comme il faut.

"Mais come along. We will be late."

PART SECOND

I

"Sing, nigger, sing! Sing yo' rhyme!
De waters is a-floodin'—dey 's a-roarin' on time!
Climb, squirrel, climb!"

For several miles, when the night was still or the wind favorable, one could follow the song, accented by simultaneous blows of implements of defense marking the measure.

"Sing, nigger, sing! Sing an' pray!
Ol' Death is on de water—he's a-ridin' dis way!
Pray, nigger, pray!"

Some of the words might have been elusive had they been unfamiliar, but the annual agitation kept the songs of the river in mind; and even in safe sections, where many sat in peace beside the rising waters, they would take their pipes from their lips to catch up the danger-songs and sympathetically pass them along. Many a prayer went with them, too, from humble petitioners who knew whereof they prayed.

Such were an old black couple who sat one night upon the brow of the outer levee at Carrollton, since become an upper district of far-reaching New Orleans.

In strong contrast to the stirring scenes enacting below the city, all was peace and tranquillity here. A strong, new embankment, securely built several hundred feet inland, had some years before supplanted the outer levee, condemned as insecure, so that the white inhabitants of the suburb slept, intelligently safe behind a double barrier, for the condemned bank had stood the stress of so many seasons that much of the low land lying between the two levees was finally occupied by squatters, mostly negroes, this being free space, taking no rent of such as did not fear the ever-impending mortgage which the river held.

Of this class, quite apart from others, might have been seen almost any evening the old couple, Hannah and Israel, sitting upon the brow of the levee near the door of their low cabin, while, always within call, there played about them a fair-haired little girl and a dog.

When the beautiful child, followed by the dog, a fine Irish setter, would suddenly emerge in a chase from among the woodpiles about the cabin, there was a certain high-bred distinction in them both which set them apart from the rest of the picture.

Sometimes they would "play too hearty," as Mammy expressed it, and she would call: "Dat 'll do now, Blossom! Come lay down, Blucher!" and, followed closely by the dog, the child would coddle at the knees of the woman, who "made the time pass" with stories. Sometimes these would be folk-tales brought over from Africa, or reminiscences of plantation life, but more often, feeling her religious responsibility to the little one, old Hannah would repeat such Bible stories as "befitted a child's mind," such as "Ab'um an' Isaac," "Eden's Gyarden," or "De Prodigum Son."

Of them all, the Eden story was easily favorite, its salient mystery features affording fine scope for the narrator's power, while they held the imaginative child with the spell of all good wonder-tales. We get these stories so young and grow up with them so familiarly that when we finally come into a realization of them they hold no possible surprise and so their first charm is lost. Think of one story with such elements as a wonder-woman rising from a man's side while he slept—a talking serpent, persuasive in temptation as insidious in easy approaches—a flaming sword of wrath—a tree of knowledge—and the sounding voice of God as he walked through the garden "in the cool of the day"! Is not a single colloquialism of so venerable ancestry sufficient to dignify a language?

Herself a classic in that she expressed the eternal quality of maternal love incarnate, the old woman thus unconsciously passed along to the object of her devotion the best classic lore of the ages. And sunrise and sunset, star- and moon-land, and their reflection in the great water-mirror, were hers and the child's, without the asking. Nor were they lost, although to both child and woman they were only common elements in life's great benediction.

During the story-telling, which generally lasted until the sun sank across the river, but while its last rays still made "pictures of glory in the heavens" with the water's reflection,—pictures which served to illustrate many a narration, to inspire the speaker and impress a sensitive child,—the dog would stretch himself facing the two, and his intelligent and quizzical expression would sometimes make Mammy laugh in a serious place or change the drift of her story. Often, indeed, this had happened in the telling of certain animal tales which Mammy declared Blucher knew better than she and she even insisted that he occasionally winked at her and set her right when she went wrong.

In the early dusk, the old man Israel would come trudging in from the water and sometimes he would light his pipe and join Mammy's audience.

Occasionally Mammy would cook the supper in the open, upon a small charcoal furnace, and the "little Miss" would sup from a tiny low table brought from the cabin. Here she was served by the old people in turn, for they never ate until she had finished. Then the little girl was carefully undressed and sung to sleep with one of Mammy's velvet lullabies, in a dainty bed all her own, a berth which hung, shelf-like, against the wall; for the home of this incongruous family was quite as novel as the family itself.

Part of the ladies' cabin of an old Mississippi steamboat, still shabbily fine in white paint and dingy gilding, which Israel had reclaimed from an abandoned wreck, formed a wing of the building. This, which, with its furnishings, Mammy called "Blossom's lay-out," communicated by a door with a "lean-to" of weather-stained boards, whose mud chimney and homely front formed a strong contrast to the river entrance of white and gold. This grotesque architectural composite would have attracted attention at another time or place, but as one of a class, made to its need of any available material, it passed unnoticed beyond an occasional casual smile of amusement and sympathy.

It was like the composite toilets of the poor blacks during the hard times suggestively called the "reconstruction period," when old women in soldier coats and boots, topped by third-hand feathered finery, waited at the distributing-station for free rations. No one ever thought of laughing at these pathetic grotesques, technically freed but newly enslaved by bitter circumstance.

On the night with which this tale begins, when Mammy had put Blossom to sleep and tucked the mosquito-bar snugly around her, she went back to her place beside her husband, and, lighting her pipe, sat for a long time silent. This was so unusual that presently Israel said:

"What de matter wid you dis evenin', Hannah? Huccome you ain't a-talkin'?"

Hannah did not answer immediately. But after a time she said slowly:

15

"I 's jes a-speculatin', Isrul—jes speculatin'." And, after another pause, she added, quite irrelevantly:

"Is you got yo' swimp-sacks all set?"

"In co'se I is." Israel's words came through a cloud of smoke.

"An' yo' oars brung in?"

"In co'se I is!"

"An' de skift locked?"

"In co'se I is!"

"An' Blucher fed?"

"What's de matter wid you, Hannah? You reckon I gwine forgit my reg'lar business?"

The old woman smoked in silence for some minutes. Then she said:

"Isrul!"

"What you want, Hannah?"

"I say, Isrul, I got some'h'n' on my mind. Hit 's been on my mind more 'n a yeah, an' hit 's a-gittin' wuss."

"What is it, Hannah?"

"You an' me we 's growin' ole, Isrul—ain't dat so?"

"Yas, Hannah."

"An' we ain't got long to stay heah, hey, Isrul?"

"Yas, ol' 'oman—can't dispute dat."

"An'"—hesitatingly. "You knows what 's on my mind, Isrul!"

"Hit 's on my mind, too, Hannah. You don't need to 'spress yo'se'f. Hit 's on my mind, day an' night."

"What's on yo' mind, Isrul?"

The old man began stirring the bowl of his pipe absently.

"'Bout we gittin' ol', Hannah, an' maybe some day we'll drap off an' leave Marse Harol's chile all by she se'f, like de chillen in de wilderness.

"What mek you mek me say it, Hannah? You knows what 'sponsibility Gord done laid on we two. Ain't we done talked it over a hond'ed times 'fo' now?"

"Dat ain't all what 's on my mind, Isrul."

"What else is you got to fret yo'se'f about, Hannah? Ain't I mekin' you a good livin'? Ain't you had de money to put a new little silk frock away every yeah for de Blossom, and ain't dey all folded away, one a-top de yether, 'g'inst de answer to our prayers, so her daddy'll see her dressed to her station when he comes sudden? Ain't you got a one-way-silk alapaca frock an' a good bonnet for yo'se'f to tek de chile by de han' wid—when Gord see fitten to answer us? You ain't hongry—or col', is yer?"

"G' way, Isrul! Who's studyin' about victuals or clo'es! I 's ponderin' about de chile, dat 's all. 'T ain't on'y 'bout we gittin' ol'. She 's gittin' tall. An' you know, Isrul, you an' me we ain't fitten to raise Marse Harol's chile. She's big enough to study quality manners an' white behavior. All Marse Harol's fam'ly's chillen knowed all de fancy high steps an' played scales on de pianner wid bofe hands at once-t, time dey was tall as Blossom is—an' dey made dancin'-school curtsies, too. I taken notice, Blossom is sort o' shy, an' she gittin' so she'll stand off when anybody speaks to her. Dis heah cabin on de river-bank ain't no place for my white folks. I sho' is pestered to see her gittin' shy an' shamefaced—like po' folks. Modest manners and upright behavior is her portion. I know it by heart, but I can't show it to her—I know it by knowledge, but of co'se I can't perform it; an' it frets me."

"Hannah!"

"What is it, Isrul?"

17

"Who gi'n us dis 'sponsibility? Is we axed for it?"

"No, Isrul, we ain't axed for it."

"Ain't you an' me promised Mis' Agnes, de day she died, to keep his chile, safe-t an' sound, tell Marse Harol' come?"

"Dat 's six yeahs past, dis comin' Christmus, Isrul. I b'lieve Marse Harol' done dead an' gone."

"Huccome you believe he dead? Is he come to you in de sperit?"

"No, he ain't come, an' dat 's huccome hope stays wid me. If he was free in de sperit lan' he sho' would come an' gimme a sign. But reason is reason, an' ef he ain't dead, huccome he don't come an' look arter his chile? My white folks warn't nuver shirkers—nor deserters. So, when I stays off my knees awhile an' casts away faith in de unseen, seem dat my horse-sense hit gives me trouble. An' den, like to-night, somehow my courage sinks, an' look like I kin see him dead an' forgot in some ol' ditch on de battle-field.

"Jes s'posin' dat 's de trufe, Isrul, what we boun' to do wid Blossom?"

"Hannah!"

"Yas, Isrul."

"You done heared a plenty o' preachin', ain't yer?"

"Yas, Isrul."

"Is you ever heared a preacher preach 'bout s'posin'?"

"No, Isrul."

"But I tell you what you is hearn 'em preach about. You hearn 'em preach about watchin' an' prayin'."

"Dat 's so, Isrul, but yit'n still, you know de scripture say 'Hope referred meketh de heart sick.' You ricollec' dat, don't you?"

18

"Yas, but dat 's a side-track. Dat ain't got nothin' to do wid answer to prayer. Dat 's jes to give comfort to weary souls, when de waitin'-time is long; dat 's all. Dey may git sick at heart—jes' waitin'."

"You right, Isrul."

"Well, an' arter watchin' an' prayin', dey 's one mo' thing needful. An' dat 's faith.

"Ef we watches for Marse Harol' to come, an' prays for 'im to come, an' don't trus', you reckon Gord gwine to bother wid us?"

"I tries to trus', Isrul, an' mos' days I does look for Marse Harol'. Many 's de time I done taken Blossom by de hand an' walked along de levee an' looked down in de Ca'ollton gyarden while de ban' played, an' jes fairly scroochinized my ol' eyes out, hopin' to reconnize 'im in de dance. I'm dat big a fool in faith—I sho' is. An' I tries de best I kin to keep my faith warm, so de good Lord 'll see it glowin' like a live coal in my heart an' he 'll 'member hisse'f about de chile an' sen' 'er daddy home, sen' 'er daddy home! My Gord, I say, SEN' 'ER DADDY HOME! I tries continu'sly, Isrul."

"You must n't talk about tryin', Hannah. You mus' jes b'lieve it, same as a little chile—same like you see it; an' den you does see it. An' when you git along so fur dat you sees wid de neye o' faith, Gord 'll sho' mek yo' faith good. Ef faith kin h'ist a mountain an' shove it along, hit can fetch a man home whar he b'longs; an' hit 'll do it, too."

"Isrul!"

"What is it, Hannah?"

"Gord ain't nuver promised to sen' Marse Harol' home, as I knows on."

"He's promised to answer de prayer o' faith, ain't He?"

"Yas, Isrul, dat 's so. Pray Him to strenken my faith, ol' man. You stays so much on de water wid de sky in yo' eyes, whilst I works 'mongst de woodpiles, so close to de yearth—seem like maybe you mought git nigher to Gord 'n what

I'm enabled to do. Pickin' up chips, hit 's lowly work an' hit keeps yo' face down, an'—"

"Don't say dat, ol' 'oman! Use yo' fo'sight an' 'stid o' you seein' chips you'll see kindlin'-wood. Dat what dey is. Dey 'll lead yo' heart upward dat-a-way. Heap o' folks don't see nothin' but money in de river—money an' mud; an' dey don't know it's a merror sometimes, full o' stars an' glory. I done read Gord's rainbow promises on de face o' dat muddy river more 'n once-t, when I lifted out my swimp-nets on a still mornin' whilst de sun an' de mist consulted together to show a mericle to a ol' dim-eyed nigger."

"You sho' does help me when you 'splains it all out dat-a-way, Isrul. Pray like a gordly man, ol' pardner, an' yo' ol' 'oman she gwine talk faith strong as she kin—widout turnin' hycoprite."

"Dat's right, honey—ol' 'oman—dat's right. You pray an' I'll pray—an' we'll watch wid faith. An' ef Gord don't sen' Marse Harol', He'll git a message to us some way, so we'll be guided."

The sound of a horn from across the river put an end to the conversation. Some one was blowing for the ferryman.

"Pity you tied Wood-duck up so soon to-night," said the old wife, following Israel with her eyes as she spoke, while he rose slowly and taking the oars down from the rafters started to the river.

In a moment the old man's answering horn sounded clear and loud in response, and the clank of the chain as it dropped in the bow of the skiff, followed by the rhythmic sound of the oar-locks, told his listening mate that the ferryman was on his way.

II

Besides plying the ferry-skiff at which Israel earned odd dimes—every day a few—he turned many an honest penny with his shrimp-nets.

The rafts of logs chained together at the landing were his, and constituted the initial station of a driftwood industry which was finally expressed in the long piles of wood which lay stacked in cord measures on either side of the cabin.

The low and prolonged talk of the old people to-night had been exceptional only in its intensity. The woman's reluctant almost despair of a forlorn hope was pathetic indeed. Still it was but momentary. They had gone over the same ground many times before, and fear and even foreboding had occasionally clouded their vision in reviewing the situation.

The woman's observation in regard to the child's growing tall was the first suggestion to Israel's mind of the urgency of immediate relief. In the stress of material provision, men may be forgiven if they sometimes overlook life's abstract values.

Israel was so startled by this new thought that when he had rowed his boat out into the clearing which the broad river afforded, he involuntarily pressed the handles of his oars, lifting their blades from the water, while he turned his eyes in one direction and another and then upward. He had a hard problem to solve. Here was a great thinking space, and yet, although he stopped for the length of several strokes, and the night was mild and still,—although every condition was favorable for clear thought,—his mind seemed lost in a sort of maze, and it was only when he discovered by a familiar landmark that he was drifting fast down-stream, only with this obtrusion of the actual, that he rallied quickly, and with a deft stroke or two recovered his course. And as the oar-locks measured time again he chuckled:

"I got my lesson, yas, I got my lesson. Work! Dat 's my po'tion. Quick as I gits biggoty and tries to read above my head, I goes de downward way."

He said it aloud, to himself, and the words gave him renewed energy, for, even as he spoke, the Duck, with oars for wings, plunged lightly forward over the water to a quickened measure.

The old wife, sitting alone, sleepless always when her man was making a night trip, was even before his summons to-night painfully awake. It was as if the outcry which had burst the door of patience had set her old mind free to wander. She seemed to have a broader vision, a new perspective upon a situation in which she was herself the chief conserving factor. While she kept the child within her door well in her subconscious care, and knew by her regular breathing that she slept: while she felt the near presence of the dog on guard at her skirts' hem, her conscious thoughts were far away.

Quickly even as lightning darts, zigzagging a path of light from one remote point to another in its eccentric course—her dim eyes actually resting upon the night skies where the lightnings play—she traveled again in her musings the arbitrary paths of fate from one crisis to another in the eventful latter years of her life. Then she would seem to see clear spaces, and again the bolts of misfortune which presaged the storm of sorrow out of which had come her present life.

First in the anxious retrospect there was the early break in the family when the boys began going away to college; then the sudden marriage of the youngest of the three; the declaration of war; the enlistment of the two elder students in the voluntary service which had transferred their names from the university roster to the list of martyrs.

Another dart as of lightning, and she saw this youngest come home with his fair New England bride, to depart with her and Israel for an island home beyond the canebrakes, and on the heel of this divided joy came his passionate enlisting "to avenge the death of his brothers." And then—ah! and then—how fast the zigzags dart! Rapid changes everywhere traced in fire, and, as memory recalled them, throughout the whole was ever the rolling thunder of artillery, completing the figure.

The story is one of thousands, individualized, of course, each, by special incidents and personalities, but the same, every one, in its history of faithfulness of the slave people during the crucial period when the masters had gone to battle, leaving their wives and babies in the care of those whose single chance of freedom depended on the defeat of the absent.

Hannah and Israel had been loved and trusted servants in the family of old Colonel Le Duc. The woman had nursed all the babies in turn, Harold being the last, and hence her own particular "baby" for all time.

Brake Island, so called because of its situation in a dense cane-brake, which was at once a menace and a guard, was the most unpopular part of the colonel's large estate, albeit there was no land so rich as its fields, no wood better stocked with game than the narrow forest lying close along its northern limit, no streams more picturesque in their windings or better equipped for the angler's art than that of the Bayou d'Iris, whose purple banks declared the spring while the robins were calling, and before the young mocking-birds in the crape myrtles opened their great red mouths for the wriggling song-food of the bayou's brim.

All the Le Duc sons had loved to go to the island to shoot and to fish while they were lads, but upon attaining the social age they had grown to despise it for its loneliness. The brake which fringed its borders had long been a refuge for runaway negroes, who were often forced to poach upon its preserves for food, even to the extent of an occasional raid upon its smoke-houses and barns, so that women and children were wont to shudder at the very idea of living there. Still it had always been the declared "favorite spot on earth" to the colonel, who had often vowed that no son of his should own it and spurn it.

He lived like a lord himself, it is true, on a broader place of less beauty on the bank of the great river,—"keeping one foot in New Orleans and one on the plantation," as he expressed it,—and it is not surprising that his children had laughingly protested against being brought up on house-parties and the opera as preparation for a hermit's life, even in "Paradise."

All excepting Harold. While the brothers had protested against the island home, he had said little, but when he had brought his bride home, and realized the scant affection that stirred the hearts of his family at sight of her placid New England face, even while he himself suffered much, knowing that her brothers were enlisting in the opposing armies and that her family felt her marriage at this time to a slaveholder as a poignant sorrow—while the father seemed hesitating as to just what paternal provision he should make for his impulsive boy, the boy himself, in a sudden towering declaration of his manhood and of resentment and pride, turned upon him:

"Give us Brake Island and Mammy and Israel, and cut us loose! And I'll show my people a new variety of hermit life!"

The thing was quickly done. A deed of gift made on the spot conveyed this Eden of modern times, with its improvements, full working force and equipment, to Harold Guyoso Le Duc, who in accepting it assumed the one condition of making it his home.

III

Harold was a brilliant fellow, impulsive and extravagant as he was handsome and loving, and he had no sooner taken possession of his Eden than he began to plan, by means of a system of engineering, to open it up by a canal which should "span the brake and tap the bayou," so that boats of size and circumstance might enter. Here he would have a launch and a barge, and the great world of culture, of wit, of pleasure, and of affluence should come in splendor "to watch a hermit herm," or, as he as often put it, "to help a hummit hum."

A great house-party was quickly arranged—a party of gay friends, engineers chiefly, bidden for a freely declared purpose—a party which is still cherished in the annals of local social history as a typical example of affluent ante-bellum hospitality, and is even yet personally recalled by a few old men who sit and seem to wait, mostly, in shabby clothing incongruously ill fitting their gilded reminiscence, at certain dozing business resorts in old New Orleans.

Most of these venerables still live in their shabby ancestral homes, although it may be their women take boarders or their best rooms are let for business purposes—cleared of their cumbersome furnishings of mahogany and rosewood by the rising waters of misfortune which have gradually carried them into the "antique-shops" of the vicinity.

A place of honor on the tax-lists and a waiting palace of white marble in the cemetery—these querulous witnesses to distinction and of permanency are in some cases the sole survivors of the many changes incident upon a reconstruction.

To these gentle reminiscers the "Brake Island house-party of Harold Le Duc" is even yet the Procrustean bed against which they measure all the ostentatious pageantry of a new and despised social order.

For the possible preservation of a bit of local color—gone out in the changed light of a new dispensation—behold a hasty sketch of this long-ago playtime. The invitations which were sent out, naming a single date only, with the flattering implication that the visit so urgently desired might never come to an end,—one of the easy fashions of the old régime,—promptly brought a dozen men, with as many women, wives and sweethearts, to the "big house" beyond the swamp.

This Southern home, which was broadly typical of its class, simple enough in its architecture in that its available space, barring the watch-tower in the center of its roof, was all upon a single floor and its material the indigenous woods of the forest, yet suffered no diminution in being called the "big house"—a name which has been made to serve many a lesser structure for purposes of distinction.

Set high upon brick pillars,—there are no cellars possible in the Mississippi valley country,—its low, spreading form graced the easy eminence upon which it stood, dominating its wide demesne with a quiet dignity superior to that of many a statelier home.

In design it was a Greek cross. Surrounded on all sides by deep balconies, ornate with cornice and Corinthian columns, its four arms afforded as many entrances, of which the southern portal was formal front, from which an avenue of arbor-vitæs led down to the canopied landing at the bayou's bank at the foot of the decline.

The house had been designed and built by Harold's father, in an exuberance of youthful enthusiasm, upon his early marriage. He it was who had planted the trailing roses and wistaria-vines, whose gnarled trunks, now woody and strong as trees, topped the balconies, throwing profusions of bloom adown their pillars and along their balustrades. Here Lamarque, Solfaterre, Cloth-of-gold, Musk-cluster, Lady-bank, Multi-flora—all the cherished climbing roses of an earlier period—mingled in harmonious relations with honeysuckle, woodbine, and clematis.

The most beautiful of them all, the single yellow-centered Cherokee rose of the soil,—good enough in itself for anywhere, but ostracized through caste exclusion from distinction of place about the home,—lay in heavy tangles in the tall, impenetrable hedges which bounded the garden on three sides meeting the bayou at the base of the knoll.

Within its inclosure a resident colony of choice flowers—exotics mainly, but domiciled and grown hardy in this protected spot—had waxed riotous in the license of years of neglect, and throwing off traditions, as many another aristocrat in like circumstances has done before, appeared now in novel forms developed in life's open race with children of the soil.

26

Here in season were great trees of camellia, white and red, with each a thousand waxen blooms, stalwart woody growths of lemon-verbena, topping sweet olives and answering the challenge of the stately oleanders, which, in turn, measured heads against the magnolias' shoulders.

Appropriating any available support, great scarlet geraniums ten feet high, knowing no winters, laid hands upon the trellises and matched pennies with the locust blooms, red petal against white, affiliating, weak-spined as they were, with scrub-trees which counted real trees at least in their Louisiana pedigrees.

"Cape jasmine borders" had risen into hedges, fencing in certain beds, while the violets, which originally guarded fantastic forms in outline, had gregariously spread into perennial patches of green and purple.

And everywhere there were orange-trees—not a grove here, but always one or more in the range of vision. Their breath was over the garden, and even the bees in the locust-trees, with all their fuss and scattering of honey sweets, could not dispel their all-pervading suggestion of romance—the romance of life incarnate ever expressed in their peerless exhibits of flower, fresh fruit and yellow, all growing together upon a maternal tree rich in life and tone.

Too many words about an old garden? Perhaps so, and yet—

The spirit of a venerable garden as it rises and shows itself to memory is such a benediction that one seeing the vision may sometimes wonder if, if life, per se, be eternal, and the resurrection of certain so-called "dead" a fact, we may not some day wander again in the risen gardens of our childhood, recognizing them by verification of certain familiar faces of flowers who may know us in turn and bloom again—taking up life, which ever includes love and immortality, at the point of suspension, as a mother, waking from a nap, goes back to her window, and catching up her broken song held in the cobwebs of sleep, sings it through, while she finishes a little sleeve, her foot again upon the cradle at her side.

Life is the great serial—one chapter printed here, another there—a seemingly finished comedy crowding a tragedy unrelated, yonder.

The discerning artist who, reading as he runs, brings these parts into line will have begun the great book. Until Gabriel wills, it may not be finished.

IV

It was, no doubt, but natural that the man of the world, who had deserted such an Eden of his own designing for the ostensible excuse of business convenience, should have resented in his sons their inherited repugnance to the retired life.

What more formidable combatant than one's own stubbornness, turned to confront him, in his children?

The broken trip from New Orleans to the Island took nearly two days, although the crow does it easily in a few hours.

The initial munificence of chartering one of the great Mississippi steamboats for the first stage of the journey set the pace for the entire occasion. Host and hostess met their guests at the river landing with carriages and cane wagons gaily bedecked with evergreens, mosses, and dogwood branches in flower, and a merry drive through several miles of forest brought them to the banks of the bayou, where a line of rowboats awaited them.

The negro boatmen, two to man each skiff, wearing jumpers of the Harvard crimson, stood uncovered in line at the bayou's edge, and as the party alighted, they served black coffee from a fire in the open.

The negro with a cup of coffee his own hue and clear as wine is ever an ubiquitous combination in the Louisiana lowlands. He bobs up so unexpectedly in strange places balancing his tiny tray upon his hand, that a guest soon begins to look for him almost anywhere after an interval of about three dry hours, and with a fair chance of not being disappointed.

When finally the party had embarked, the hostess riding in the first boat with the governor of the State, while Harold brought up the rear with the governor's lady, the sun was low in the west, and narrow search-lights, piercing the wood for a brief moment, revealed a great wonder-world of dank growths so fairly alive with creeping, flying, darting things—chirping, calling, singing, croaking, humming, and hooting—that when in a twinkling the light suddenly went out, many of the women shuddered with a shrinking sense of the uncanny.

Before this intangible emotion had time to crystallize into fear, however, each pilot who manipulated the rudder astern had drawn from under his seat a great torch of pine and set it ablaze.

Under festoons of gray Spanish moss, often swung so low that heads and torches were obliged to defer to them, and between flowering banks which seemed sometimes almost to meet in the floating growths which the dividing bows of the boats plowed under, the little crafts sped lightly along.

Occasionally a heavy plunging thing would strike the water with a thud, so near a boat that a girlish shriek would pierce the wood, spending itself in laughter. A lazy alligator, sleepily enjoying a lily-pool, might have been startled by the light, or a line of turtles, clinging like knots to a log over the water, suddenly let go.

Streaks of darting incandescence marked the eccentric flights of a million fireflies flecking the deep wood whose darkness they failed to dispel; and once or twice two reflected lights a few inches apart, suggesting a deer in hiding, increased the tremulous interest of this super-safe but most exciting journey.

But presently, before impressions had time to repeat themselves, and objects dimly discerned to become familiar, a voice from the leading boat started a song.

It was a great voice, vibrant, strong, and soft as velvet, and when presently it was augmented by another, insidiously thrown in, then another in the next boat, until all the untutored Harvard oarsmen were bravely singing and the dipping oars fell into the easy measure, all sense of fear or place was lost in the great uplift of the rhythmic melody.

At special turns through the wood ringing echoes gave back the strains. A mocking-bird, excited by the unusual noise, poured forth a rival disputatious song, and an owl hooted, and something barked like a fox; but it was the great singing of the men which filled the wood.

Common songs of the plantation followed one another—songs of love, of night and bats, of devils and hobgoblins, selected according to the will of the leader— all excepting the opening song, which, although of the same repertoire, was "by request," and for obvious reasons.

It was called "When de Sun Swings Low," and ran something like this:

Look out for Mister Swaller when de sun swings low—
Watch him swoop an' sway!
He keeps a mighty dippin', like he don' know whar to go,
A-saggin' every way.
He starts sort o' nimbly,
But he settles mighty wimbly
When he scurries for de chimbley
When de sun swings low.
Does you see a cloud a-risin' when de sun swings low?
Listen ef it sings.
Hit 's a swarm o' gray muskitties, 'bout a million strong or so,
A-sharpenin' up der stings.
Dey keeps a mighty filin',
An' dey tries to sing beguilin',
But de 'skitties' song is rilin'
When de sun swings low.
Oh, de woods is all conversin' when de sun swings low—
Bird an' beast an' tree;
Dey all communes together in de languages dey know,
An' sperits rise to see.
De nightmares prances,
An' de will-o'-wisp dances,
When de moonlight advances
An' de sun swings low.
But most naïve and characteristic of them all perhaps was "Ol' Marse Adam."

Ole Mister Devil took a walk in Paradise—
Lady Mis' Eve she's a-walkin', too—
Hoped to meet Mars' Adam, she was steppin' mighty nice—
Lady Mis' Eve she's a-walkin', too.
Dis was 'fo' de fig-time, so my lady picked a rose—
Lady Mis' Eve she's a-walkin', too—
An' she helt it 'g'inst de sunlight, as she felt de need o' clo'es—
Lady Mis' Eve she's a-walkin', too.
Den she shuk 'er yaller ringlets down an' 'lowed dat she was dressed—
Lady Mis' Eve, she's a-walkin', too—
Mister Devil he come quoilin'—everbody knows de rest—
Lady Mis' Eve she's a-walkin', too.

Then, changing to a solemn, staccato measure, it went on:

Ole Marse Adam! Ole Marse Adam!
Et de lady's apple up an' give her all de blame.
Greedy-gut, greedy-gut, whar is yo' shame?
Ole Marse Adam, man, whar is yo' shame?
Ole Marse Adam! Ole Marse Adam!
Caught de apple in 'is neck an' made it mighty so'e,
An' so we po' gran'chillen has to swaller roun' de co'e.
Ole Marse Adam, man, whar is yo' shame?
Ole Marse Adam! Ole Marse Adam!
Praised de lady's attitudes an' compliment 'er figur'—
Didn't have de principle of any decent nigger.
Ole Marse Adam, man, whar is yo' shame?

It was a long pull of five miles up the winding stream, but the spirit of jollity had dispelled all sense of time, and when at last the foremost boat, doubling a jutting clump of willows, came suddenly into the open at the foot of the hill, the startling presentment of the white house illuminated with festoons of Chinese lanterns, which extended across its entire width and down to the landing, was like a dream of fairyland.

It was indeed a smiling welcome, and exclamations of delight announced the passage of the boats in turn as they rounded the willow bend.

The firing of a single cannon, with a simultaneous display of fireworks, and music by the plantation band, celebrated the landing of the last boat.

Servants in the simple old-fashioned dress—checked homespun with white accessories, to which were added for the occasion, great rosettes of crimson worn upon the breast—took care of the party at the landing, bringing up the rear with hand-luggage, which they playfully balanced upon their heads or shifted with fancy steps.

The old-time supper—of the sort which made the mahogany groan—was served on the broad back "gallery," while the plantation folk danced in the clearing beyond, a voice from the basement floor calling out the figures.

This was a great sight.

Left here to their own devices as to dress, the negroes made so dazzling a display that, no matter how madly they danced, they could scarcely answer the challenge of their own riotous color schemes.

Single dancers followed; then "ladyes and gentiles" in pairs, taking fantastic steps which would shame a modern dancing-master without once awakening a blush in a maiden's cheek.

The dancing was refined, even dainty, to-night, the favorite achievement of the women being the mincing step taken so rapidly as to simulate suspension of effort, which set the dancers spinning like so many tops, although there was much languid posing, with exchange of salutations and curtsying galore.

Yet not a twirl of fan or dainty lift of flounce—to grace a figure or display a dexterous foot—but expressed a primitive idea of high etiquette.

The "fragments" left over from the banquet of the upper porch—many of them great unbroken dishes, meats, game, and sweets—provided a great banquet for the dancers below, and the gay late feasters furnished entertainment, fresh and straight from life, to the company above, for whose benefit many of their most daring sallies were evidently thrown out—and who, after their recent experiences, were pleased to be so restfully entertained.

Toasts, drunk in ginger-pop and persimmon beer innocent of guile, were offered after grace at the beginning of the supper, the toaster stepping out into the yard and bowing to the gallery while he raised his glass or, literally, his tin cup—the passage of the master's bottle among the men, later in the evening, being a distinct feature.

The first toast was offered to the ladies—"Mistus an' Company-ladies"; and the next, following a suggestion of the first table, where the host had been much honored, was worded about in this wise:

"We drinks to de health, an' wealth, an' de long life of de leadin' gentleman o' Brake Island, who done put 'isself to so much pains an' money to give dis party. But to make de toast accordin' to manners, so hit'll fit de gentleman's visitors long wid hisself, I say let's drink to who but 'Ole Marse Adam!'"

It is easy to start a laugh when a festive crowd is primed for fun, and this toast, respectfully submitted with a low bow by an ancient and privileged veteran of the rosined bow, was met with screams of delight.

V

A resourceful little island it was that could provide entertainment for a party of society folk for nearly a fortnight with never a repetition to pall or to weary.

The men, equipped for hunting or fishing, and accompanied by several negro men-servants with a supplementary larder on wheels,—which is to say, a wagon-load of bread, butter, coffee, condiments, and wines, with cooking utensils,—left the house early every morning, before the ladies were up.

They discussed engineering schemes over their fishing-poles and game-bags, explored the fastnesses of the brake, eavesdropped for the ultimate secret of the woods, and plumbed for the bayou's heart, bringing from them all sundry tangible witnesses of geologic or other conditions of scientific values.

Most of these "witnesses," however, it must be confessed, were immediately available for spit or grill, while many went—so bountiful was the supply—to friends in the city with the cards of their captors.

There are champagne bottles even yet along the marshes of Brake Island, bottles whose bellies are as full of suggestion as of mud, and whose tongueless mouths fairly whistle as if to recount the canards which enlivened the swampland in those halcyon days of youth and hope and inexperience.

Until the dressing-hour, in the early afternoons which they frankly called the evening, the young women coddled their bloom in linen cambric night-gowns, mostly, reading light romance and verse, which they quoted freely under the challenge of the masculine presence.

Or they told amazing mammy-tales of voudoo-land and the ghost-country for the amused delectation of their gentle hostess, who felt herself warmed and cheered in the sunshine of these Southern temperaments. It seemed all a part of the poetry and grace of a novel and romantic life.

Here were a dozen young women, pretty and care-free as flowers, any one of whom could throw herself across the foot of a bed and snatch a superfluous "beauty-sleep" in the midst of all manner of jollity and laughter.

Most of them spoke several languages and as many dialects, frequently passing from one to another in a single sentence for easy subtlety or color, and with distinct gain in the direction of music.

Possibly they knew somewhat of the grammar of but a single tongue beside their own, their fluency being more of a traditional inheritance than an acquisition. Such is the mellow equipment of many of our richest speakers.

Not one but could pull to pieces her Olympe bonnet and nimbly retrim it with pins, to match her face or fancy—or dance a Highland fling in her 'broidered nightie, or sing—

How they all did sing—and play! Several were accomplished musicians. One knew the Latin names of much of the flora of the island, and found time and small coins sufficient to interest a colony of eager pickaninnies to gather specimens for her "herbarium."

Without ever having prepared a meal, they could even cook, as they had soon amply proven by the heaping confections which were always in evidence at the man-hour—bon-bons, kisses, pralines, what not?—all fragrant with mint, orange-flower, rose-leaf, or violet, or heavy with pecans or cocoanut.

In the afternoon, when the men came home, they frequently engaged in contests of skill—in rowing or archery or croquet; or, following nature's manifold suggestions, they drifted in couples, paddling indolently among the floating lily-pads on the bayou, or reclining among the vines in the summer-houses, where they sipped iced orange syrup or claret sangaree, either one a safe lubricator, by mild inspiration or suggestion, of the tongue of young love, which is apt to become tied at the moment of most need.

"Sipped iced orange syrup or claret sangaree"

With the poems of Moore to reinforce him with easy grace of words, a broad-shouldered fellow would naïvely declare himself a peri, standing disconsolate at the gate of his lady's heart, while she quoted Fanny Fern for her defense, or, if she were passing intellectual and of a broader culture, she would give him invitation in form of rebuff from "The Lady of the Lake," or a scathing line from

Shakspere. Of course, all the young people knew their Shakspere—more or less.

They had their fortunes told in a half-dozen fashions, by withered old crones whose dim eyes, discerning life's secrets held lightly in supension, mated them recklessly on suspicion.

Visiting the colored churches, they attended some of the novel services of the plantation, as, for instance, a certain baptismal wedding, which is to say a combined ceremony, which was in this case performed quite regularly and decorously in the interest of a coal-black piccaninny, artlessly named Lily Blanche in honor of two of the young ladies present whom the bride-mother had seen but once out driving, but whose gowns of flowered organdy, lace parasols, and leghorn hats had stirred her sense of beauty and virtue to action.

Although there was much amusement over this incongruous function, the absence of any sense of embarrassment in witnessing so delicate a ceremony— one which in another setting would easily have become indelicate—was no doubt an unconscious tribute to the primitive simplicity of the contracting parties.

And always there were revival meetings to which they might go and hear dramatic recitals of marvelous personal "experiences," full of imagery,—travels in heaven or hell,—with always the resounding human note which ever prevails in vital reach for truth. Through it all they discerned the cry which finds the heart of a listener and brings him into indissoluble relation with his brother man, no matter how great the darkness out of which the note may come. It is universal.

The call is in every heart, uttered or unexpressed, and one day it will pierce the heavens, finding the blue for him who sends it forth, and for the listener as well if his heart be attuned.

Let who will go and sit through one of these services, and if he does not come away subdued and silent, more tender at heart, and, if need be, stronger of hand to clasp and to lift, perhaps—well, perhaps his mind is open only to the pictorial and the spectacular.

There is no telling how long the house-party would have remained in Paradise but for the inexorable calendar which warned certain of its members that they would be expected to answer the royal summons of Comus at the approaching carnival; and of course the important fact that certain bills from the legislature affecting the public weal were awaiting the governor's signature.

A surprising number of marriages followed this visit, seeming to confirm a report of an absurd number of engagements made on the island.

There is a certain old black woman living yet "down by the old basin" in French New Orleans, a toothless old crone who, by the irony of circumstance, is familiarly known as "Ol' Mammy Molar," who "remembers" many things of this time and occasion, which she glibly calls "de silveringineer party," and who likes nothing better than an audience.

If she is believed, this much too literal account of a far-away time is most meager and unfaithful, for she does most strenuously insist that, for instance, there was served at the servants' table on that first night—

But let her have her way of it for a moment—just a single breath:

"Why, honey," she closes her eyes as she begins, the better to see memory behind them. "Why, honey, de champagne wine was passed aroun' to de hands all dat indurin' infair in water-buckets, an' dipped out in gou'd dippers-full, bilin' over so fast an' fizzin' so it'd tickle yo' mouf to drink it. An' Marse Harol' Le Duc, he stood on a pianner-stool on de back gallery an' th'owed out gol' dollars by de hatful for any of us niggers to pick up; an' de guv'ner, ol' Marse Abe Lincolm, he fired off sky-rockers an' read out freedom papers.

"An' mids' all de dance an' reveltry, a bolt o' thunder fell like a cannon-ball outen a clair sky, an' we looked up an' lo an' beholst, here was a vision of a big hand writin' on de sky, an' a voice say, 'Eat up de balance ef anything is found wantin'!' an' wid dat, dey plunged in like a herd o' swine boun' for de sea, an' dey devoured de fragmints an' popped mo' corks, an' dipped out mo' champagne wine, an' de mo' dey dipped out champagne wine, de mo' dey 'd dance. An' de mo' dey 'd dance, de mo' de wine would flow."

Possibly the old woman's obvious confusion of thought has some explanation in the fact of the presence of the governor of the State, who, introduced as a high dignitary, did make a little speech late that night, thanking the colored people in terms of compliment for their dancing; and any impression made here was so quickly overlaid by the deeper experiences of the war that a blending can easily be explained.

There was a shower of coins—"picayunes" only—thrown during the evening by the master, a feature of the dance being to recover as many of them as possible without breaking step. So the old woman's memory is not so far afield, although as a historian she might need a little editing. But such even as this is much of the so-called "history" which, bound in calf, dishonors the world's libraries to-day.

It is so easy, seeing cobwebs upon a record,—cobwebs which may not be quite construed as alphabet,—to interpret them as hieroglyphics of import, instead of simply brushing them away, or relegating them, where they belong, to the dusky domain of the myth out of which we may expect only weird suggestion, as from the mold of pressed rosemary, typifying remembrance dead.

The house-party, which in this poor retrospect seems to have devoted itself almost wholly to pleasure, was nevertheless followed by immediate work upon the project in behalf of which it was planned.

With this main motive was also the ulterior and most proper one in Harold's mind of introducing his wife in so intimate a fashion to some of the important members of society, who would date life-friendships from the pleasant occasion of helping him to open his own door to them.

Some thousands of dollars went into the quicksands of the marshes before the foundations were laid for the arch of a proposed great bridge, beneath which his boats should sail to their landing. With the arrogant bravado of an impulsive boy challenged to action, he began his arch first. Its announcement of independence and munificence would express the position he had taken. Sometimes it is well to put up a bold front, even if one needs work backward from it.

Harold moved fast—but the gods of war moved faster!

Scarcely had a single column of solid masonry risen above the palmetto swamp when Fort Sumter's guns sounded. The smell of gunpowder penetrated the fastnesses of the brake, and yet, though his nostrils quivered like those of an impetuous war-horse, the master held himself in rein with the thought of her who would be cruelly alone without him. And he said to himself, while he reared his arch: "Two out of three are enough! I have taken their terror island for my portion. They may have garlands upon my bridge—when they come sailing up my canal as heroes!"

But the next whiff from the battleground stopped work on the arch. The brothers had fallen side by side.

"The brave, unthinking fellow, after embracing his beloved, dashed to the front"

Madly seizing both the recovered swords, declaring he would "fight as three," the brave, unthinking fellow, after embracing his beloved, put one of her hands in Hannah's and the other in Israel's, and, commending them to God by a speechless lift of his dark eyes, mounted his horse and dashed, as one afraid to look back, to the front.

VI

Every one knows the story of "poor Harold Le Duc"—how, captured, wounded, he lay for more than a year on the edge of insanity in a Federal hospital. Every one knows of the birth of his child on the lonely island, with only black hands to receive and tend it, and how the waiting mother, guarded by the faithful two, and loved by the three hundred loyal slaves who prayed for her life, finally passed out of it on the very day of days for which she had planned a great Christmas banquet for them in honor of their master's triumphant return.

The story is threadbare. Everyone knows how it happened that "the old people," Colonel and Madame Le Duc, having taken flight upon report of a battle, following their last son, had crossed the lines and been unable from that day to communicate with the island; of the season of the snake-plague in the heart of the brake, when rattlers and copperheads, spreading-adders, moccasins, and conger-eels came up to the island, squirming, darting, or lazily sunning themselves in its flowering grounds and lily-ponds, some even finding their way into the very beds of the people; when the trees were deserted of birds, and alligators prowled across the terraces, depredating the poultry-yard and even threatening the negro children.

In the presence of so manifold disaster many of the negroes returned to voodooism, and nude dances by weird fires offered to Satan supplanted the shouting of the name of Christ in the churches. A red streak in the sky over the brake was regarded as an omen of blood—the thunderbolt which struck the smoke-stack of the sugar-house a command to stop work.

Old women who had treated the sick with savory teas of roots and herbs lapsed into conjuring with bits of hair and bones. A rabbit's foot was more potent than medicine; a snake's tooth wet with swamp scum and dried in the glare of burning sulphur more to be feared than God.

War, death and birth and death again, followed by scant provender threatening famine, and then by the invasion of serpents, had struck terror into hearts already tremulous and half afraid.

The word "freedom" had scarcely reached the island and set the air vibrating with hope, commingled with dread, when the reported death of the master came as a grim corroboration of the startling prospect.

41

All this is an open story.

But how Israel and Hannah, aided in their flight by a faithful few, slipped away one dark night, carrying the young child with them to bear her safely to her father's people, knowing nothing of their absence, pending the soldier's return—for the two never believed him dead; how, when they had nearly reached the rear lands of the paternal place, they were met by an irresistible flood which turned them back; and how, barely escaping with their lives, they were finally rowed in a skiff quite through the hall of the great house—so high, indeed, that Mammy rescued a family portrait from the wall as they passed; how the baby slept through it all, and the dog followed, swimming—

This is part of the inside history never publicly told.

The little party was taken aboard a boat which waited midstream, a tug which became so overcrowded that it took no account of passengers whom it carried safely to the city. Of the poor forlorn lot, a few found their way back to the plantations in search of survivors, but in most instances, having gone too soon, they returned disheartened.

Madame Le Duc, who, with her guests and servants, had fled from the homestead at the first warning, did not hear for months of the flight of the old people with her grandchild, and of their supposed fate. No one doubted that all three had perished in the river, and the news came as tardy death tidings again—tidings arriving after the manner of war news, which often put whole families in and out of mourning, in and out of season.

VII

There is not space here to dwell upon Harold's final return to Brake Island, bent and broken, unkempt,—disguised by the marks of sorrow, unrecognized, as he had hoped to be, of the straggling few of his own negroes whom he encountered camping in the wood, imprisoned by fear. These, mistaking him for a tramp, avoided him. He had heard the news en route,—the "news," then several years old,—and had, nevertheless, yielded to a sort of blind, stumbling fascination which drew him back to the scene of his happiness and his despair. Here, after all, was the real battle-field—and he was again vanquished.

When he reached the homestead, he found it wholly deserted. The "big house," sacred to superstition through its succession of tragedies, was as Mammy and Israel had left it. Even its larder was untouched, and the key of the wine-cellar lay imbedded in rust in sight of the cob-webbed door.

It was a sad man, prematurely gray, and still gaunt—and white with the pallor of the hospital prison—who, after this sorrowful pilgrimage to Brake Island, appeared, as from the grave, upon the streets of New Orleans. When he was reinstated in his broken home, and known once more of his family and friends, he would easily have become the popular hero of the hour, for the gay world flung its gilded doors open to him.

The Latin temperament of old New Orleans kept always a song in her throat, even through all the sad passages of her history; and there was never a year when the French quarter, coquette that she was, did not shake her flounces and dance for a season with her dainty toes against the lower side of Canal Street.

But Harold was not a fellow of forgetful mind. The arch of his life was broken, it is true, but like that of the bridge he had begun—a bridge which was to invite the gay world, yes, but which would ever have dominated it, letting its sails pass under—he could be no other than a worthy ruin. Had his impetuous temper turned upon himself on his return to the island, where devastation seemed to mock him at every turn, there is no telling where it might have driven him. But a lonely mother, and the knowledge that his father had died of a broken heart upon the report of his death, the last of his three sons—the pathetic, dependence of his mother upon him—the appeal of her doting eyes and the exigencies of an almost hopeless financial confusion—all these combined as a challenge to his manhood to take the helm in the management of a wrecked estate.

It was a saving situation. How often is work the great savior of men!

Once stirred in the direction of effort, Harold soon developed great genius for the manipulation of affairs. Reorganization began with his control.

Square-shouldered and straight as an Indian, clear of profile, deep-eyed, and thoughtful of visage, the young man with the white hair was soon a marked figure. When even serious men "went foolish over him," it is not surprising that ambitious mothers of marriageable daughters, in these scant days of dearth of men, should have exhibited occasional fluttering anxieties while they placed their broken fortunes in his hands.

Reluctantly at first, but afterward seeing his way through experience, Harold became authorized agent for some of the best properties along the river, saving what was left, and sometimes even recovering whole estates for the women in black who had known before only how to be good and beautiful in the romantic homes and gardens whose pervading perfume had been that of the orange-blossom.

It was on returning hurriedly from a trip to one of these places on the upper river—the property of one Marie Estelle Josephine Ramsey de La Rose, widowed at "Yellow Tavern"—that he sought the ferry skiff on the night old man Israel answered the call.

VIII

Little the old man dreamed, while he waited, midstream, trying to think out his problem, that the solution was so near at hand.

We have seen how the old wife waited and prayed on the shore; how with her shaded mind she groped, as many a wiser has done, for a comforting, common-sense understanding of faith, that intangible "substance of things hoped for," that elusive "evidence of things not seen."

In a moment after she heard the creaking of the timbers as the skiff chafed the landing, even while she rose, as was her habit, to see who might be coming over so late, she dimly perceived two men approaching, Israel and another; and presently she saw that Israel held the man's hand and that he walked unsteadily.

She started, fearing that her man was hurt; but before she could find voice of fear or question, Israel had drawn the stranger to her and was saying in a broken voice:

"Hannah! Hannah! Heah Mars' Harol'!"

Only a moment before, with her dim eyes fixed upon the sky, she had experienced a realization of faith, and believed herself confidently awaiting her master's coming. And yet, seeing him now in the flesh before her, she exclaimed:

"What foolishness is dis, ole man? Don't practice no jokes on me to-night, Isrul!"

Her voice was almost gruff, and she drew back as she spoke. But even while she protested, Harold had laid his hand upon her arm.

"Mammy," he whispered huskily, "don't you know your 'indurin' devil'—?" (This had been her last, worst name for her favorite during his mischief period.)

Harold never finished his sentence. The first sound of his voice had identified him, but the shock had confused her. When at last she sobbed "Hush! I say, hush!" her arms were about his knees and she was crying aloud.

45

"Her arms were about his knees"

"Glo-o-o—oh—glo-o-o—glo-o-ry! Oh, my Gord!" But presently, wiping her eyes, she stammered: "What kep' you so, Baby? Hol' me up, chile—hol' me!"

She was falling, but Harold steadied her with strong arms, pressing her into her chair, but retaining her trembling hand while he sat upon the low table beside her.

He could not speak at once, but, seeing her head drop upon her bosom, he called quickly to Israel. For answer, a clarion note, in no wise muffled by the handkerchief from which it issued, came from the woodpile. Israel was shy of his emotions and had hidden himself.

By the time he appeared, sniffling, Hannah had rallied, and was pressing Harold from her to better study his face at long range.

"What happened to yo' hair, Baby?" she said presently. "Hit looks as bright as dat flaxion curl o' yoze I got in my Testamen'. I was lookin' at it only a week ago las' Sunday, an' wishin' I could read de book 'long wid de curl."

"It is much lighter than that, Mammy. It is whiter than yours. I have lived the sorrows of a long life in a few years."

Israel still stood somewhat aside and was taking no note of their speech, which he presently interrupted nervously:

"H-how you reckon Mars' Harol' knowed me, Hannah? He—he reco'nized his horn! You ricollec' when I fotched dat horn f'om de islan' roun' my neck, clean 'crost de flood, you made game o' me, an' I say I mought have need of it? But of co'se I didn't ca'culate to have it ac-chilly call Mars' Harol' home! I sho' didn't! But dat's what it done. Cep'n' for de horn's call bein' so familius, he'd 'a' paid me my dime like a stranger an' passed on."

At this Harold laughed.

"Sure enough, Uncle Israel; you didn't collect my ferriage, did you? I reckon you'll have to charge that."

Israel chuckled:

"Lord, Hannah, listen! Don't dat soun' like ole times? Dey don't charge nothin' in dese han'-to-mouf days, Marse Harol'—not roun' heah."

"But tell me, Uncle Israel, how did you happen to bring that old horn with you—sure enough?" Harold interrupted.

"I jes fotched it 'ca'se I couldn't leave it—de way Hannah snatched yo' po'trit off de wall—all in dat deluge. Hit's heah in de cabin now to witness de trip. But in co'se o' time de horn, hit come handy when I tuk de ferry-skift.

"Well, Hannah, when he stepped aboa'd, he all but shuk de ole skift to pieces. I ought to knowed dat Le Duc high-step, but I didn't. I jes felt his tread, an' s'luted him for a gentleman, an' axed him for Gord sake to set down befo' we'd be capsided in de river. I war n't cravin' to git drownded wid no aristoc'acy.

"De moon she was hidin', dat time, an' we couldn't see much; but he leant over an' he say, 'Uncle,' he say, 'who blowed dat horn 'crost de river?' An' I say, 'Me, sir. I blowed it.' Den he say, 'Whose horn is dat?' An' I 'spon', 'Hit's my horn, sir.' Den my conscience begin to gnaw, an' I sort o' stammered, 'Leastways, it b'longs to a frien' o' mine wha' look like he ain't nuver gwine to claim it.' I ain't say who de frien' was, but d'rec'ly he pushed me to de wall. He ax me p'intedly to my face, 'What yo' frien' name, uncle?' An at dat I got de big head an' I up an' snap out:

"'Name Le Duc, sir, Harry Le Duc.'

"Jes free an' easy, so, I say it. Lord have mussy! Ef I'd s'picioned dat was Mars' Harol' settin' up dar listenin' at me callin' his name so sociable an' free, I'd 'a' drapped dem oa's overbo'ad. I sho' would.

"Well, when I say 'Harry Le Duc,' seem like he got kind o' seasick, de way he bent his head down, an' I ax him how he come on—ef he got de miz'ry anywhars. An' wid dat he sort o' give out a dry laugh, an' den what you reckon he ax me? He say, 'Uncle, is you married?' An' wid dat I laughed. 'T war n't no trouble for me to laugh at dat. I 'spon', 'Yas, sirree! You bet I is! Does I look like air rovin' bachelor?' I was jes about half mad by dis time.

"Well, so he kep' on quizzifyin' me: ax me whar I live, an' I tol' 'im I was a ole risidenter on de levee heah for five years past; an' so we run on, back an' fo'th, tell we teched de sho'. An' time de skift bumped de landin' he laid his han' on me an' he say, 'Unc' Isrul, whar's Mammy Hannah?' An' den—bless Gord! I knowed him! But I ain't trus' myself to speak. I des nachelly clawed him an' drug him along to you. I seen de fulfilment o' promise, an' my heart was bustin' full, but I ain't got no halleluiah tongue like you. I jes passed him along to you an' made for de woodpile!"

It was a great moment for Harold, this meeting with the only people living who could tell all there was to know of those who were gone.

Hannah's memory was too photographic for judicious reminiscence. The camera's great imperfection lies in its very accuracy in recording non-essentials, with resulting confusion of values. So the old woman, when she turned her mental search-light backward, "beginning at the beginning," which to Harold seemed the end of all—the day of his departure,—recounted every trivial incident of the days, while Harold listened through the night, often suffering keenly in his eagerness to know the crucial facts, yet fearing to interrupt her lest some precious thing be lost.

A reflected sunrise was reddening the sky across the river when she reached the place in the story relating to the baby. Her description needed not any coloring of love to make it charming, and while he listened the father murmured under his breath:

"And then to have lost her!"

"What dat you say, Marse Harol'?" Hannah gasped, her quick ears having caught his despairing tone.

"Oh, nothing, Mammy. Go on. It did seem cruel to have the little one drowned. But I don't blame you. It is a miracle that you old people saved yourselves."

The old woman turned to her husband and threw up her hands.

"Wh-why, Isrul!" she stammered.

"What's de matter wid you—to set heah all night an' listen at me talkin' all roun' de baby—an' ain't named her yit!"

She rose and, drawing Harold after her, entered the door at her back. As she pulled aside the curtain a ray of sunlight fell full upon the sleeping child.

"Heah yo' baby, Baby!" Her low voice, steadied by its passages through greater crises, was even and gentle.

She laid her hand upon the child.

"Wek up, baby! Wek up!" she cried. "Yo' pa done come! Wek up!"

Without stirring even so much as a thread of her golden hair upon the pillow, the child opened a pair of great blue eyes and looked from Mammy's face to the man's. Then,—so much surer is a child's faith than another's,—doubting not at all, she raised her little arms.

Her father, already upon his knees beside her, bent over, bringing his neck within her embrace, while he inclosed her slender body with his arms. Thus he remained, silent, for a moment, for the agony of his joy was beyond tears or laughter. But presently he lifted his child, and, sitting, took her upon his lap. He could not speak yet, for while he smoothed her beautiful hair and studied her face, noting the blue depths of her darkly fringed eyes, the name that trembled for expression within his lips was "Agnes—Agnes."

"How beautiful she is!" he whispered presently; and then, turning to Hannah, "And how carefully you have kept her! Everything—so sweet."

"Oh, yas!" the old woman hastened to answer. "We ain't spared no pains on 'er, Marse Harol'. She done had eve'ything we could git for her, by hook or by crook. Of co'se she ain't had no white kin to christen her, an' dat was a humiliation to us. She didn't have no to say legal person to bring 'er for'ard, so she ain't nuver been ca'yed up in church; but she's had every sort o' christenin' we could reach.

"I knowed yo' pa's ma, ole Ma'am Toinette, she'd turn in her grave lessen her gran'chil' was christened Cat'lic, so I had her christened dat way. Dat ole half-blind priest, Father Some'h'n' other, wha' comes from Bayou de Glaise, he was conductin' mass meetin' or some'h'n' other, down here in Bouligny, an' I took de baby down, an' he sprinkled her in Latin or some'h'n' other, an' ornamented behind her ears wid unctious ile, an' crossed her little forehead, an' made her eat a few grains o' table salt. He done it straight, wid all his robes on, an' I g'in him a good dollar, too. An' dat badge you see on her neck, a sister o' charity, wid one o' dese clair-starched ear-flap sunbonnets on, she put dat on her. She say she give it to her to wear so 's she could n't git drownded—like as ef I'd let her drownd. Yit an' still I lef' it so, an' I even buys a fresh blue ribbin for it, once-t an'a while. I hear 'em say dat blue hit's de Hail Mary color—an' it becomes her eyes, too. Dey say what don't pizen fattens, an' I know dem charms couldn't do her no hurt, an', of 'co'se, we don't know all. Maybe dey mought ketch de eye of a hoverin' angel in de air an' bring de baby into Heavenly notice. Of co'se, I wouldn't put no sech as dat on her. I ain't been raised to it, an' I ain't no beggin' hycoprite. But I wouldn't take it off, nuther.

"Den, I knowed ole Mis', yo' ma, she was 'Pistopal, an' Miss Aggie she was Numitarium; so every time a preacher'd be passin' I'd git him to perform it his way. Me bein' Baptis' I didn't have no nigger baptism to saddle on her.

"So she's bounteously baptized—yas, sir. I reasoned it out dat ef dey's only one true baptism, an' I war n't to say shore which one it was, I better git 'em all, an' only de onlies' true one would count; an' den ag'in, ef all honest baptisms is good, den de mo' de merrier, as de Book say. Of co'se I knowed pyore rain-water sprinkled on wid a blessin' couldn't hurt no chile.

"You see, when one side de house is French distraction an' de yether is English to-scent, an' dey's a dozen side-nations wid blood to tell in all de branches,—well, hit minds me o' dis ba'm of a thousan' flowers dat ole Mis' used to think so much of. Hits hard to 'stinguish out any one flagrams.

"But talkin' about de baby, she ain't been deprived, no mo' 'n de Lord deprived her, for a season, of her rights to high livin' an'—an' aristoc'acy—an'—an' petigree, an' posterity, an' all sech as dat.

"An'—

"What dat you say, Mars' Harol'? What name is we—'

"We ain't dast to give 'er no name, Baby, no mo' 'n jes Blossom. I got 'er wrote down in five citificates 'Miss Blossom,' jes so. No, sir. I knows my colored place, an' I'll go so far, an' dat's all de further. She was jes as much a blossom befo' she was christened as she was arterwards, so my namin' 'er don't count. I was 'mos' tempted to call out 'Agnes' to de preachers, when dey'd look to me for a name, seem' it was her right—like as ef she was borned to it; but—I ain't nuver imposed on her. No, sir, we ain't imposed on her noways.

"De on'iest wrong I ever done her—an' Gord knows I done it to save her to my arms, an' for you, marster—de on'iest wrong was to let her go widout her little sunbonnet an' git her skin browned up so maybe nobody wouldn't s'picion she was clair white an' like as not try to wrest her from me. An' one time, when a uppish yo'ng man ast me her name, I said it straight, but I see him look mighty cu'yus, an' I spoke up an' say, 'What other name you 'spect' her to have? My name is Hannah Le Duc, an' I's dat child's daddy's mammy.' Excuse me, Mars' Harold, but you know I is yo' black mammy—an' I was in so'e straits.

"So de yo'ng man, well, he didn't seem to have no raisin'. He jes sort o' whistled, an' say I sho is got one mighty blon' gran'chil'—an' I 'spon', 'Yas, sir; so it seems.'

"An' dat's de on'ies' wrong I ever done her. She sets up at her little dinner-table sot wid a table-cloth an' a white napkin,—an' I done buyed her a ginuine silver-plated napkin-ring to hold it in, too,—an' she says her own little blessin'—dat short 'Grace o' Gord—material binefets,' one o' Miss Aggie's; I learned it to her. No, she ain't been handled keerless, ef she is been livin' on de outside o' de levee, like free niggers. But we ain't to say lived here, 'not perzackly, marster. We jes been waitin' along, so, dese five years—waitin' for to-night.

"I ain't nuver sorted her clo'es out into no bureau; I keeps 'em all in her little trunk, perpared to move along."

For a moment the realization of the culmination of her faith seemed to suffuse her soul, and as she proceeded, her voice fell in soft, rhythmic undulations.

"Ya-as, Mars' Harol', Mammy's baby boy, yo' ol' nuss she been waitin', an' o-ole man Isrul he been waitin', an' de Blossom she been waitin'. I 'spec' she had de firmes' faith, arter all, de baby did. Day by day we all waited—an' night by night. An' sometimes when courage would burn low an' de lamp o' faith grow dim, seem like we'd a' broke loose an' started a-wanderin' in a sort o' blind search, 'cep'n' for de river.

"Look like ef we'd ever went beyan' de river's call, we'd been same as de chillen o' Isrul lost in de tanglement o' de wilderness. All we river chillen, we boun' to stay by her, same as toddlin' babies hangs by a mammy's skirts. She'll whup us one day, an' chastise us severe; den she'll bring us into de light, same as she done to-night—same as reel mammies does.

"An', Mars' Harol'—"

She lowered her voice.

"Mars' Harol', don't tell me she don't know! I tell yer, me an' dis River we done spent many a dark night together under de stars, an' we done talked an' answered one another so many lonely hours—an' she done showed us so many mericles on land an' water—

"I tell yer, I done found out some'h'n' about de River, Mars' Harol'. She's—why, she's—

"Oh, ef I could only write it all down to go in a book! We been th'ough some merac'lous times together, sho' 's you born—sho' 's you born.

"She's a mericle mystery, sho'!

"You lean over an' dip yo' han' in her an' you take it up an' you say it's wet. You dig yo' oars into her, an' she'll spin yo' boat over her breast. You dive down into her, an' you come up—or don't come up. Some eats her. Some drinks her. Some gethers wealth outen her. Some draps it into her. Some drownds in her.

"An' she gives an' takes, an' seem like all her chillen gits satisfaction outen her, one way an' another; but yit an' still, she ain't nuver flustered. On an' on she goes—rain or shine—high water—low water—all de same—on an' on.

"When she craves diamonds for her neck, she reaches up wid long onvisible hands an' gethers de stars out'n de firmamint.

"De moon is her common breastpin, an' de sun—

"Even he don't faze her. She takes what she wants, an' sends back his fire every day.

"De mists is a veil for her face, an' de showers fringes it.

52

"Sunrise or dusklight, black night or midday, every change she answers whilst she's passin'.

"But who ever inticed her to stop or to look or listen? Nobody, Baby. An' why?

"Oh, Lord! ef eve'ybody only knowed!

"You see, all sech as dat, I used to study over it an' ponder befo' we started to talk back an' fo'th—de River an' me.

"One dark night she heared me cryin' low on de bank, whilst de ole man stepped into de boat to row 'crost de water, an' she felt Wood-duck settle heavy on her breast, an' she seen dat we carried de same troublous thought— searchin' an' waitin' for the fulfilment o' promise.

"An' so we started to call—an' to answer, heart to heart."

The story is nearly told. No doubt many would be willing to have it stop here. But a tale of the river is a tale of greed, and must have satisfaction.

While father and child sat together, Israel came, bringing fresh chips. He had been among the woodpiles again. This time there followed him the dog.

"Why, Blucher!" Harold exclaimed. "Blucher, old fellow!" And at his voice the dog, whining and sniffing, climbed against his shoulder, even licking his face and his hand. Then, running off, he barked at Israel and Hannah, telling them in fine dog Latin who the man was who had come. Then he crouched at his feet, and, after watching his face a moment, laid his head upon his master's right foot, a trick Harold had taught him as a pup.

IX

Of course Harold wished to take the entire family home with him at once, and would hear to nothing else until Hannah, serving black coffee to him from her furnace, in the dawn, begged that she and Israel might have "a few days to rest an' to study" before moving.

It was on the second evening following this, at nightfall, while her man was away in his boat, that the old woman rose from her chair and, first studying the heavens and then casting about her to see that no one was near, she went down to the water, slowly picking her way to a shallow pool between the rafts and the shore. She sat here at first, upon the edge of the bank, frankly dropping her feet into the water while she seemed to begin to talk—or possibly she sang, for the low sound which only occasionally rose above the small noises of the rafts was faintly suggestive of a priest's intoning.

For a moment only, she sat thus. Then she began to lower herself into the water, until, leaning, she could lay her face against the sod, so that a wave passed over it, and when, letting her weight go, she subsided, with arms extended, into the shallow pool, a close listener might have heard an undulating song, so like the river's in tone as to be separable from it only through the faint suggestion of words, interrupted or drowned at intervals by the creaking and knocking of the rafts and the gurgling of the sucking eddies about them.

The woman's voice—song, speech, or what not?—seemed intermittent, as if in converse with another presence.

Suddenly, while she stood thus, she dropped bodily, going fully under the water for a brief moment, as if renewing her baptism, and when she presently lifted herself, she was crying aloud, sobbing as a child sobs in the awful momentary despair of grief at the untwining of arms—shaken, unrestrained.

While she stood thus for a few minutes only,—a pathetic waste of sorrow, wet, dark and forlorn, alone on the night-shore,—a sudden wind, a common evening current, threw a foaming wave over the logs beside her so that its spray covered her over; while the straining ropes, breaking and bumping timbers, with the slow dripping of the spent wave through the raft, seemed to answer and possibly to assuage her agitation; for, as the wind passed and the waters subsided, she suddenly grew still, and, climbing the bank as she had come, walked evenly as one at peace, into her cabin.

No one will ever know what, precisely, was the nature of this last communion. Was it simply an intimate leave-taking of a faithful companionship grown dear through years of stress? Or had it deeper meaning in a realization—or hallucination—as to the personality of the river—the "secret" to which she only once mysteriously referred in a gush of confidence on her master's return?

Perhaps she did not know herself, or only vaguely felt what she could not tell. Certainly not even to her old husband, one with her in life and spirit, did she try to convey this mystic revelation. We know by intuition the planes upon which our minds may meet with those of our nearest and dearest. To the good man and soldier, Israel,—the prophet, even, who held up the wavering hands of the imaginative woman when her courage waned, pointing to the hour of fulfilment,—the great river, full of potencies for good or ill, could be only a river. As a mirror it had shown him divinity, and in its character it might typify to his image-loving mind another thing which service would make it precious. But what he would have called his sanity—had he known the word—would have obliged him to stop there.

The stars do not tell, and the poor moon—at best only hinting what the sun says—is fully half-time off her mind. And the soul of the River—if, indeed, it has once broken silence—may not speak again.

And, so, her secret is safe—safe even if the broken winds did catch a breath, here and there, sending it flurriedly through and over the logs until they trembled with a sort of mad harp-consciousness, and were set a-quivering for just one full strain—one coherent expression of soul-essence—when the wave broke. Perhaps the arms of the twin spirits were untwined—and they went their separate ways smiling—the woman and the river.

When, after a short time, the old wife came out, dressed in fresh clothing, her white, starched tignon shining in the moonlight, to sit and talk with her husband, her composure was as perfect as that of the face of the water which in its serenity suggested the voice of the Master, when Peter would have sunk but for his word.

This was to be their last night here. Harold was to bring a carriage on the next day to take them to his mother and Blossom, and, despite the joy in their old hearts, it cost them a pang to contemplate going away. Every woodpile seemed to hold a memory, each feature of the bank a tender association. Blucher lay sleeping beside them.

Israel spoke first.

"Hannah!" he said.

"What, Isrul?"

"I ready to go home to-night, Hannah. Marse Harol' done come. We done finished our 'sponsibility—an' de big river's a-flowin' on to de sea—an' settin' heah, I 'magines I kin see Mis' Aggie lookin' down on us, an' seem like she mought want to consult wid us arter our meetin' wid Marse Harol' an' we passin' Blossom along. What you say, Hannah?"

"I been tired, ole man, an' ef we could 'a' went las' night, like you say, seem like I 'd 'a' been ready—an', of co'se, I'm ready now, ef Gord wills. Peace is on my sperit. Yit an' still, when we rests off a little an' studies freedom free-handed, we won't want to hasten along maybe. Ef we was to set heah an' wait tell Gord calls us,—He ain't ap' to call us bofe together, an' dey'd be lonesome days for the last one. But ef we goes 'long wid Marse Harol', he an' Blossom'll be a heap o' comfort to de one what's left."

"Hannah!"

"Yas, Isrul."

"We's a-settin' to-night close to de brink—ain't dat so?"

"Yas, Isrul."

"An' de deep waters is in sight, eh, Hannah?"

"Yas, Isrul."

"An' we heah it singin', ef we listen close, eh, Hannah?"

"Yas, Isrul."

"Well, don't let 's forgit it, dat 's all. Don't let's forgit, when we turns our backs on dis swellin' tide, dat de river o' Jordan is jes befo' us, all de same—an' it can't be long befo' our crossin'-time."

"Amen!" said the woman.

The moon shone full upon the great river, making a shimmering path of light from shore to shore, when the old couple slowly rose and went to rest.

Toward morning there was a quick gurgling sound in front of the cabin. Blucher caught it, and, springing out, barked at the stars. The sleepers within the levee hut slept on, being overweary.

The watchman in the Carrollton garden heard the sound,—heard it swell almost to a roar,—and he ran to the new levee, reaching its summit just in time to see the roof of the cabin as it sank, with the entire point of land upon which it rested, into the greedy flood.

When Harold Le Duc arrived that morning to take the old people home, the river came to meet him at the brim of the near bank, and its face was as the face of smiling innocence.

While he stood awe-stricken before the awful fact so tragically expressed in the river's bland denial, a wet dog came, and, whining, crouched at his feet. He barked softly, laid his head a moment upon his master's boot, moaned a sort of confidential note, and, looking into the air, barked again, softly.

Did he see more than he could tell? Was he trying to comfort his master? He had heard all the sweet converse of the old people on that last night, and perhaps he was saying in his poor best speech that all was well.

Mammy Hannah and Uncle Israel, having discharged their responsibility, had crossed the River together.

PART THIRD

"Oh, it 's windy,
Sweet Lucindy,
On de river-bank to-night,
An' de moontime
Beats de noontime,
When de trimblin' water 's white."

So runs the plantation love-song, and so sang a great brown fellow as, with oars over his shoulder, he strolled down "Lovers' Lane," between the bois d'arcs, toward the Mississippi levee.

He repeated it correctly until he neared the gourd-vine which marked the home of his lady, when he dropped his voice a bit and, eschewing rhyme for the greater value, sang:

"Oh, it 's windy,
Sweet Maria,
On de river-bank to-night—"
And slackening his pace until he heard footsteps behind him, he stopped and waited while a lithe yellow girl overtook him languidly.

"Heah, you take yo' sheer o' de load!" he laughed as he handed her one of the oars. "Better begin right. You tote half an' me half." And as she took the oar he added, "How is you to-night, anyhow, sugar-gal?"

While he put his right arm around her waist, having shifted the remaining oar to his left side, the girl instinctively bestowed the one she carried over her right shoulder, so that her left arm was free for reciprocity, to which it naïvely devoted itself.

"I tell yer, hit 's fine an' windy to-night, sho' enough," he said. "De breeze on de levee is fresh an' cool, an' de skift she's got a new yaller-buff frock, an' she—"

"Which skift? De Malviny? Is you give her a fresh coat o' paint? An' dat's my favoryte color—yaller-buff!" This with a chuckle.

"No; dey ain't no Malviny skift no mo'—not on dis plantation. I done changed her name."

"You is, is yer? What is you named her dis time?"

She was preparing to express surprise in the surely expected. Of course the boat was renamed the Maria. What else, in the circumstances?

"I painted her after a lady-frien's complexion, a bright, clair yaller; but as to de name—guess!" said the man, with a lunge toward the girl, as the oar he carried struck a tree—a lunge which brought him into position to touch her ear with his lips while he repeated: "What you reckon I named her, sweetenin'?"

"How should I know? I ain't in yo' heart!"

"You ain't, ain't yer? Ef you ain't, I'd like mighty well to know who is. You's a reg'lar risidenter, you is—an' you knows it, too! Guess along, gal. What you think de boat's named?"

"Well, ef you persises for me to guess, I'll say Silv' Ann. Dat 's a purty title for a skift."

"Silv' Ann!" contemptuously. "I 'clare, M'ria, I b'lieve you 's jealous-hearted. No, indeedy! I know I run 'roun' wid Silv' Ann awhile back, jes to pass de time, but she can't name none o' my boats! No; ef you won't guess, I'll tell yer—dat is, I'll give you a hint. She named for my best gal! Now guess!"

"I never was no hand at guessin'." The girl laughed while she tossed her head. "Heah, take dis oah, man, an' lemme walk free. I ain't ingaged to tote no half-load yit—as I knows on. Lordy, but dat heavy paddle done put my whole arm to sleep. Ouch! boy. Hands off tell de pins an' needles draps out. I sho' is glad to go rowin' on de water to-night."

So sure was she now of her lover, and of the honor which he tossed as a ball in his hands, never letting her quite see it, that she whimsically put away the subject.

She had been to school several summers and could decipher a good many words, but most surely, from proud practice, she could spell her own name. As they presently climbed the levee together, she remarked, seeing the water:

"Whar is de boat, anyhow—de What-you-may-call-it? She ain't in sight—not heah!"

"No; she's a little piece up de current—in de willer-clump. I didn't want nobody foolin' wid 'er—an' maybe readin' off my affairs. She got her new intitlemint painted on her stern—every letter a different color, to match de way her namesake treats me—in a new light every day."

The girl giggled foolishly. She seemed to see the contour of her own name, a bouquet of color reaching across the boat, and it pleased her. It would be a witness for her—to all who could read.

"I sho' does like boats an' water," she generalized, as they walked on.

"Me, too," agreed her lover; "but I likes anything—wid my chosen company. What is dat whizzin' past my face? Look like a honey-bee."

"'T is a honey-bee. Dey comes up heah on account o' de chiny-flowers. But look out! Dat's another! You started 'em time you drug yo' oah in de mids' o' dem chiny-blossoms. Whenever de chiny-trees gits too sickenin' sweet, look out for de bees!"

"Yas," chuckled de man; "an' dey's a lesson in dat, ef we'd study over it. Whenever life gits too sweet, look out for trouble! But we won't worry 'bout dat to-night. Is you 'feared o' stingin' bees?"

"No, not whilst dey getherin' honey—dey too busy. Hit 's de idlers dat I shun. An' I ain't afeared o' trouble, nuther. Yit an' still, ef happiness is a sign, I better look sharp."

"Is you so happy, my Sugar?"

The girl laughed.

"I don't know ef I is or not—I mus' see de name on dat skift befo' I can say. Take yo' han' off my wais', boy! Ef you don't I'll be 'feared o' stingin' bees, sho' enough! Don't make life too sweet!"

They were both laughing when the girl dashed ahead into the willow-clump, Love close at her heels, and in a moment the Maria, in her gleaming dress of yellow, darted out into the sunset.

A boat or two had preceded them, and another followed presently, but it takes money to own a skiff, or even to build one of the driftwood, which is free to the captor. And so most of the couples who sought the river strolled for a short space, finding secluded seats on the rough-hewn benches between the acacia-trees or on the drift-dogs which lined the water's edge. It was too warm for continued walking.

From some of the smaller vessels, easily recognizable as of the same family as the fruit-luggers which crowd around "Picayune Tier" at the French market, there issued sweet songs in the soft Italian tongue, often accompanied by the accordeon.

Young Love sang on the water in half a dozen tongues, as he sings there yet at every summer eventide.

The skiffs for the most part kept fairly close to the shore, skirting the strong current of the channel, avoiding, too, the large steamboats, whose passage ever jeopardized the small craft which crossed in their wake.

Indeed, the passage of one of these great "packets" generally cleared the midstream, although a few venturesome oarsmen would often dare fate in riding the billows in her wake. These great steamboats were known among the humble river folk more for their wave-making power than for the proud features which distinguished them in their personal relations.

There were those, for instance, who would watch for a certain great boat called the Capitol, just for the bravado of essaying the bubbling storm which followed her keel, while some who, enjoying their fun with less snap of danger, preferred to have their skiffs dance behind the Laurel Hill. Or perhaps it was the other way: it may have been the Laurel Hill, of the sphere-topped smoke-stacks, which made the more sensational passage.

It all happened a long time ago, although only about thirteen years had passed since the events last related, and both boats are dead. At least they are out of the world of action, and let us hope they have gone to their rest. An old hulk stranded ashore and awaiting final dissolution is ever a pathetic sight, suggesting a patient paralytic in his chair, grimly biding fate—the waters of eternity at his feet.

At intervals, this evening, fishermen alongshore—old negroes mostly—pottered among the rafts, setting their lines, and if the oarsmen listened keenly, they might almost surely have caught from these gentle toilers short snatches of low-pitched song, hymns mostly, of content or rejoicing.

There was no sense of the fitness of the words when an ancient fisher sang "Sweet fields beyan' de swelling flood," or of humor in "How firm a foundation," chanted by one standing boot-deep in suspicious sands. The favorite hymn of several of the colored fishermen, however, seemed to be "Cometh our fount of every blessin'," frankly so pronounced with reverent piety.

At a distant end of his raft, hidden from its owner by a jutting point from which they leaped, naked boys waded and swam, jeering the deaf singer as they jeered each passing boat, while occasionally an adventurous fellow would dive quite under a skiff, seizing his opportunity while the oars were lifted.

None of the little rowboats carried sail as a rule, although sometimes a sloop would float by with an air of commanding a squadron of the sparse fleet which extended along the length of the river.

The sun was fallen nearly to the levee-line this evening when one of the finest of the "river palaces" hove in sight.

The sky-hour for "dousing the great glim" was so near—and the actual setting of the sun is always sudden—that, while daylight still prevailed, all the steamer's lights were lit, and although the keen sun which struck her as a search-light robbed her thousand lamps of their value, the whole scene was greater for the full illumination.

The people along shore waved to the passing boat—they always do it—and the more amiable of the passengers answered with flying handkerchiefs.

As she loomed radiant before them, an aged negro, sitting mending his net, remarked to his companion:

"What do she look like to you, Br'er Jones?"

"'What she look like to me?'" The man addressed took his pipe from his lips at the question. "What she look like—to me?" he repeated again. "Why, tell the trufe, I was jes' studyin' 'bout dat when you spoke. She 'minds me o' Heaven; dat what she signifies to my eyes—Heavenly mansions. What do she look like to you?"

"Well," the man shifted the quid in his mouth and lowered his shuttle as he said slowly, "well, to my observance, she don't answer for Heaven; I tell yer dat: not wid all dat black smoke risin' outen 'er 'bominable regions. She's mo' like de yether place to me. She may have Heavenly gyarments on, but she got a hell breath, sho'. An' listen at de band o' music playin' devil-dance time inside her! An' when she choose to let it out, she's got a-a-nawful snort—she sho' is!"

"Does you mean de cali-ope?"

"No; she ain't got no cali-ope. I means her clair whistle. Hit's got a jedgment-day sound in it to my ears."

"Dat music you heah', dat ain't no dance-music. She plays dat for de passengers to eat by, so dey tell me. But I reckon dey jes p'onounces supper dat-a-way, same as you'd ring a bell. An' when de people sets down to de table, dey mus' sho'ly have de manners to stop long enough to let 'em eat in peace. Yit an' still, whilst she looks like Heaven, I'd a heap ruther set heah an' see her go by 'n to put foot in her, 'ca'se I'd look for her to 'splode out de minute I landed in her an' to scatter my body in one direction an' my soul somewhars else. No; even ef she was Heaven, I'd ruther 'speriment heah a little longer, settin' on de sof' grass an' smellin' de yearnin' trees an' listenin' at de bumblebees a-bumblin', an' go home an' warm up my bacon an' greens for supper, an' maybe go out foragin' for my Sunday chicken to-night in de dark o' de moon. Hyah! My stomach hit rings de dinner-bell for me, jes as good as a brass ban'."

"Me, too!" chuckled the smoker. "I'll take my chances on dry lan', every time. I know I'll nuver lead a p'ocession but once-t, and dat'll be at my own fun'al, an' I don't inten' to resk my chances. But she is sho' one noble-lookin' boat."

By this time the great steamboat—the wonderful apparition so aptly typifying Heaven and hell—had passed.

She carried only the usual number of passengers, but at this evening hour they crowded the guards, making a brilliant showing. Family parties they were mostly, with here and there groups of young folk, generally collected about some popular girl who formed a center around which coquetry played mirthfully in the breeze. A piquant Arcadian bride, "pretty as red shoes," artlessly appearing in all her white wedding toggery, her veil almost crushed by its weight of artificial orange-flowers, looked stoically away from the little dark husband who persisted in fanning her vigorously, while they sat in the sun-filled corner which they had taken for its shade while the boat was turned into the landing to take them aboard. And, of course, there was the usual quota of staid couples who had survived this interesting stage of life's game.

Nor was exhibition of rather intimate domesticity entirely missing. Infancy dined in Nature's own way, behind the doubtful screening of waving palmetto fans. While among the teething and whooping-cough contingents the observer of life might have found both tragedy and comedy for his delectation.

Mild, submissive mothers of families, women of the Creole middle class mainly,—old and withered at thirty-five, all their youthful magnolia tints gone wrong, as in the flower when its bloom is passed—exchanged maternal experiences, and agreed without dissent that the world was full of trouble, but "God was good."

Even a certain slight maternal wisp who bent over a tiny waxen thing upon her lap, dreading each moment to perceive the flicker in her breath which would show that a flame went out—even she, poor tear-dimmed soul, said it while she answered sympathetic inquiry:

"Oh, yas; it is for her we are taking de trip. Yas, she is very sick, mais God is good. It is de eye-teet'. De river's breath it is de bes' medicine. De doctor he prescribe it. An' my father he had las' winter such a so much trouble to work his heart, an' so, seeing we were coming, he is also here—yas, dat's heem yonder, asleep. 'T is his most best sleep for a year, lying so. De river she give it. An' dose ferryboat dey got always on board too much whooping-cough to fasten on to eye-teet."

Somewhat apart from the other passengers, their circle loosely but surely defined by the irregular setting of their chairs toward a common center, sat a group, evidently of the great world—most conspicuous among them a distinguished-looking couple in fresh mid-life, who led the animated discussion, and who were seen often to look in the direction of a tall and beautiful girl who stood in the midst of a circle of young people within easy call. It was impossible not to see that their interest in the girl was vital, for they often exchanged glances when her laughter filled the air, and laughed with her, although they knew only that she had laughed.

The girl stood well in sight, although "surrounded six deep" by an adoring crowd; nor was this attributable alone to her height which set her fine little head above most of her companions. A certain distinction of manner—unrelated to haughtiness, which may fail in effect, or arrogance, which may over-ride but never appeal; perhaps it was a graciousness of bearing—kept her admirers ever at a tasteful distance.

There was an ineffable charm about the girl, a thing apart from the unusual beauty which marked her in any gathering of which she became a part.

Descriptions are hazardous and available words often inadequate to the veracious presentment of beauty, and yet there is ever in perfection a challenge to the pen.

As the maiden stood this evening in the sunlight, her radiant yellow hair complementing the blue of her sea-deep eyes, her fair cheeks aglow, and one color melting to another in her quick movements, the effect was almost like an iridescence. Tender in tints as a sea-shell, there might have been danger of lapse into insipidity but for the accent of dark rims and curled lashes which individualized the eyes, and, too, the strong, straight lines of her contour, which, more than the note of dark color, marked her a Le Duc.

There are some women who naturally hold court, no matter what the conditions of life, and to whom tribute comes as naturally as the air they breathe. It often dates back into their spelling-class days, and I am not sure that it does not occasionally begin in the "perambulator."

This magnetic quality—one hesitates to use an expression so nervously prostrated by strenuous overwork, and yet it is well made and to hand—this magnetic quality, then, was probably, in Agnes Le Duc, the gift of the Latin strain grafted upon New England sturdiness and reserve, the one answering, as one might say, for ballast, while the other lent sail for the equable poising of a safe and brilliant life-craft.

So, also, was her unusual beauty markedly a composite and of elements so finely contrasting that their harmonizing seemed rather a succession of flashes, as of opposite electric currents meeting and breaking through the caprice of temperamental disturbance; as in the smile which won by its witchery, or the illumination with which rapid thought or sudden pity kindled her eye.

Educated alternately in Louisiana where she had recited her history lessons in French, and in New England, the pride and pet of a charmed Cambridge circle, with occasional trips abroad with her "parents," she was emerging, all unknowingly, a rather exceptional young woman for any place or time.

Seeing her this evening, an enthusiast might have likened her to the exquisite bud of a great tea-rose, regal on a slender stem—shy of unfolding, yet ultimately unafraid, even through the dewy veil of immaturity—knowing full well, though she might not stop to remember, the line of court roses in her pedigree.

Watching her so at a safe distance, one could not help wondering that she thought it worth her while to listen at all, seeing how her admirers waited upon her every utterance. To listen well has long been considered a grace—just to listen; but there is a still higher art, perhaps, in going a step beyond. It is to listen with enthusiasm, yes, even with eloquence. One having a genius for this sort of oratory, speaking through the inspired utterance of another, and of course supplying the inspiration, gains easily the reputation of "delightful conversational powers."

And this was precisely an unsuspected quality which made for the sweet girl much of the popularity which she had never analyzed or questioned. She could talk, and in several languages, familiarly, and when the invitation arrived, she did—upward, with respect, to her elders (she had learned that both in New Orleans and in Boston); downward to her inferiors—with gentle directness, unmixed with over-condescension; to right and to left among her companions, quite as a free-hearted girl, with spirit and camaraderie.

A quality, this, presaging social success certainly, and, it must be admitted, it is a quality which sometimes adorns natures wanting in depth of affection. That this was not true of Agnes Le Duc, however, seems to be clearly shown in an incident of this trip.

As she stood with her companions this evening, while one and another commented upon this or that feature of the shore, they came suddenly upon a congregation of negroes encircling an inlet between two curves in the levee, and, as the low sun shone clearly into the crowd, it became immediately plain that a baptism was in progress.

A line of women, robed in white, stood on one side; several men, likewise in white, on the other, while the minister, knee-deep in the water, was immersing a subject who shouted wildly as he went under and came up struggling as one in a fit, while two able-bodied men with difficulty bore him ashore.

The scene was scarcely one to inspire reverence to a casual observer, and there was naturally some merriment at its expense. One playful comment led to another until a slashing bit of ridicule brought the entire ceremony into derision, and, as it happened, the remark with its accompanying mimicry was addressed to Agnes.

"Oh, please!" she pleaded, coloring deeply. "I quite understand how it may affect you; but—oh, it is too serious for here—too personal and too sacred—"

While she hesitated, the culprit, ready to crawl at her feet,—innocent, indeed, of the indelicacy of which he had become technically guilty,—begged to be forgiven. He had quite truly "meant no harm."

"Oh, I am quite sure of it," the girl smiled; "but now that I have spoken,—and really I could not help it; I could not wish to let it pass, understand,—but now that I have spoken—oh, what shall I say!

"Perhaps you will understand me when I tell you that I should not be with you here to-day but for the devoted care of two old Christian people who dated their joy in the spiritual life from precisely such a ceremony as this. They are in Heaven now.

"My dear old Mammy often said that she 'went under the water groaning in sin, and came up shouting, a saved soul!' I seem to hear her again as I repeat the words, on this same river, in sight of her people and within the sound of their voices. I was small when she died, and I do not clearly remember many of her words; but this I do well recall, for we lived for some years on the river-bank, only a few miles from the spot where in her youth she had been immersed. She taught me to love the river, and perhaps I am a little sentimental over it. I hope always to be so. My father remembers many of her words. She was his nurse, too. She told him as a boy that she had insisted on being baptized in flowing water, so that her sins might be carried away to the sea. It was all very sacred to her."

Of course the romantic story of Agnes's youth was known to every one present, and this unexpected allusion awakened immediate interest.

"Oh, yes," she replied to a question; "I suppose I do remember a good deal, considering how very young I was, and yet I often wonder that I do not remember more, as it was all so unusual;" and then she added, laughing: "I seem to forget that no event could surprise a child in her first experiences of life. Yet I remember trivial things, as, for instance, the losing of a hat. I clearly recall our watching my hat on one occasion when it blew into the river, and was never recovered! Think of the tragedy of it! I can see it now, tossing like a little boat, as it floated away.

"And the funny little cabin I remember—I know I do, for there were things which papa never saw, on the inside, in what he calls my 'boudoir,' the white cabin, which I shall never forget. When anything is kept ever in mind by constant description, it is hard to know how much one really remembers. You know, papa spent only one night there and his thoughts were turned backward, so that he naturally kept only vague impressions of the place.

"Yes, he has made a sketch of it from memory, and I am sorry. Why? Oh, because I was sure at first that it was not correct, and now it has come to stand to me in place of the true picture, which has faded. It is a way with pictures if we let them over-ride us. Why, my grandmother in Boston has a friend who had his wife's portrait painted after she was lost at sea. He spent all the money he had to have it done by a 'best artist who had made a hasty sketch of her in life,' and when it came home he did not recognize it—really thought a mistake had been made. Then, seeing that it was she as authoritatively pictured, and that he had paid his all to get it, he bethought him to study it, hoping some day to find her in it. And so he did, gradually.

"He had it hung over his smoking-table, and every evening he scrutinized it until its insistence conquered. For a whole year he lived in the companionship of an absent wife as seen in an artist's mood (this last sentence is a direct quotation from my Boston grandmama, who is fond of the story). And—well, 'what happened?' Why, this: One day the woman came home. People 'lost at sea' occasionally do, you know. And would you believe it? Her widower—I mean to say her husband—refused to receive her. He did not know her! He simply pointed to the painting and shook his head. And if she hadn't been a person of resolution and resource,—descended from the Mayflower,—why, she would have had to go away. But she had her trunk brought in and quietly paid the expressman and took off her bonnet—and stayed. But it was an absurdly long time before her husband was wholly convinced that he was not the victim of an adventuress. And she says that even now he sometimes looks at her in a way she does not like.

"So, you see, we cannot always believe our own eyes, which are so easily tricked.

"Still, even knowing all this, we consent to be duped. Now I like the picture of the cabin, even while I regret it, and, although I know better, I accept it.

"What is truth, anyway? That is what you hear said so often in Boston, where we are said to try to make pivots of it for the wheels of all our little hobbies.

"'Do I like Boston?' Like Boston? No. I adore it! Oh, yes! But yet, when I am there, I am a little rebel. And at each place I am quite honest, I assure you. You see, I have a grandmother at both places—here and there. Such dears, they are—adorable, both, and so different!

"Yes, that is true. Papa's portrait, the one Mammy had in the cabin,—yes, we have it,—twice recovered from the river. My father offered a reward, and a man brought it out of the mud, a little way down the levee, and not seriously hurt. It is a funny little picture of papa at six, in a Highland costume, with his arm over a strange dog which belonged to the artist. He looks in the picture as if he were stuffed—the dog does; but papa denies that. I believe this same dog appeared in most of the portraits done by this man, in all of those of boys, at least. For the girls he supplied a cat, or occasionally a parrot. The bird was stuffed, I believe. He did my stepmother at five, and she holds the cat. The portraits hang side by side now. If we could find him, and the parrot, he should paint me, and we would start a menagerie.

"Oh, yes; going back to the subject, there are many little things which I remember, without a doubt, for I could never imagine them. For instance, I remember at least one of my baptisms—the last, I suppose. I know I was frightened because the minister shouted, and Mammy kept whispering to me that he wouldn't harm me; and then he suddenly threw water all over me and I bawled. No, I have no idea who he was; but it was out of doors, and there was a rooster in it someway. I suppose it was on the levee and the rooster came to see what was happening.

"There is a picture which always reminds me of the time we lived behind the woodpiles, that called 'The Soldier's Dream,' in which a poor fellow, asleep on the battle-field, sees dimly, as in the sky, a meeting between himself and his family.

"I am sure that while we sat on the levee and Mammy talked to me of papa's coming, I used to picture it all against the sunset sky. Just look at it now. Was anything ever more gorgeous and at the same time so tender? One could easily imagine almost any miracle's happening over there in the west.

"Yes, I know the skies of Italy, and they're no better. They are bluer and pinker, perhaps, in a more paintable way; but when the sun sets across the Mississippi, especially when we have their dreamy cloud effects, it goes down with variation and splendor unmatched anywhere, I do believe. But," she added with a Frenchy shrug, "you know I am only a river child, and everything belonging to the old muddy stream is dear to me.

"I beg your pardon—what did you ask?" This to a very young man who colored after he had spoken. "Did we ever recover—? Oh, no. Their bodies went with the waters they loved—and it was better so. Certainly, papa used every effort. I hope the current carried them to the sea. She would have liked to have it so, I am sure, dear, dear Mammy Hannah!

"Oh, yes. The little monument on Brake Island is only 'in memory,' as its inscription says."

This was rather thoughtful talk for a girl scarcely eighteen, but Agnes had ever been thoughtful, and by common inheritance—from her mother and her father.

As the scene shifted, and conversation passed to lighter things, and her laughter rippled again as a child's, its range was sometimes startling. It was as brilliant as a waterfall seen in the sun, and often while her fond father watched her, as now, he wondered if, perchance, her laughter might not be prophetic of a great career for which eyes less devoted than his perceived her eminently fitted.

It is beyond the province of this tale of the river to follow Agnes Le Duc through life. Some day, possibly, her story may be fully told; but perhaps a foreshadowing of her future, in one phase of it at least, may be discerned in an intimation let fall by one of the passengers who sat with his companions at a card-table in the fore cabin. At least, they had spent the day there, stopping not even for dinner, and now they were moving away. As they found seats out on the guards, he was saying:

"'Rich!' Well, I would say so! He own all doze plantation around de town of Waterproof, and de strange part is he paid twice for some of dem! Of co'se he could not do such a so-foolish t'ing except he made dat invention. When you begin to collec' so much on every one of anyt'ing dat fill a want, you get rich, sure!

"No matter if it jus' one picayune—when dey sell enough. Dey say you can make sugar so quick by dat machine he invent—it is like conjuring—a sort of hoodoo!"

"Yes," said his companion, an American, "so I understand; and there is no man I would rather see rich than Harold Le Duc. His marriage, so soon after the recovery of his child, surprised some of us, but no doubt it was a good thing."

"A good t'ing! It was magnificent! If he is one of de finest men in Louisiana, she is equal to him. Dat remark dat he married only for a mudder for his child—dat's all in my heye! I am sure he was in love to her one year, maybe two, befo' dat—mais, I am not sure he would have asked any woman to marry him. He had not de courage. For him love was past—and he was afraid of it. Mais de chil' she wake him up again! Oh, it is a good t'ing, sure! An' de strange part, she t'ought she wou'n' never love again, jus' de same as him—until—"

"Until what?"

"Well, until he spoke! Until what you t'ink?"

"Nothing. I t'ought maybe it was somet'ing unusual."

"Well, an' is dat not somet'ing unusual—when a widow is sure she will not love again? Dey often t'ink so, mais she was absolutely sure! You see, her first husband he was one hero; he fell on de same battle-field wid gallant 'Jeb'

Stuart—from a stray shot when de fighting was over, carrying dat poor imbecile, Philippe Delmaire, off de fiel', biccause he was yelling so, wid dat one li'l' toe he los'! A good fellow, yas, mais no account! Yas, he drank himself to deat', all on account for de loss of dat toe, so he say. Excuses dey are cheap, yas. If it was not his toe it would have been somet'ing else. You know, his figure, it was really perfection, no mistake, an' to lose perfection, even in so small a matter as one toe—it prey on his mind. Tell de trut', I used to feel sorry for him, an'—an'—when he always would touch his glass an' drink dat favorite toast, 'To my big toe!' well, dere was somet'ing pitiful in it. I used to drink it wid him. It was no harm, an' he had always good wine, poor fellow. Mais to t'ink of Paul de La Rose dying for him! It make me mad, yet when I t'ink so, I am almos' sorry to reflect I have drunk to his toe! Bah—a valu'ble man—to die like dat! Wat you say? Yas, da's true. It makes not how de soldier fall—de glory is de same. Well, any'ow, if he could have picked out a successor, he could not have done better dan yo'ng Le Duc—sure! What you say? ''Ow is he bought doze plantation twice?' Well, dis way: When he had to take dem on mortgage, an' dey were sold at de door of de court-house—bidding against him, understand—no rainy-day sale—he paid double—I mean to say he paid so much as de mortagage again. Not in every case, mais in many—to widows. I know two cousin of mine, he paid dem so. I ricollec' dey tol' me dat he was de mos' remembering man to look out for dem, an' de mos' forgetting to sen' de bills.

"Oh, yas. An' his daughter, dey say she is in love to her stepmother—an' she is jus' so foolish about de chil'—an' wid good reason. She had never children—an' she is proud for dat daughter, an' jealous, too, of dose Yankee rillation. Still, she invite dem to come every year, so the chil' can stay—an' now, would you believe it? Dey are come to be great friends, mais, of co'se, her father sends her every year at Boston to her grandmother. Dey all want her, an' no wonder. If she was one mud fence, I suppose it would be all de same, mais you know, she is one great beauty! I say one gr-r-r-reat beauty! Wh! An'when I whistle so 'wh!' I mean what I say. You see me so, I am one ol' man, now—pas' forty—an' rich in children, an' not bad-looking children, neither; mais I would walk, me, all de way from de barracks up to Bouligny, an' back, just to see her pass in de street an' smile on me. You take my word, if she is not snapped up by some school-boy, she can marry anyt'ing—a coronet! An' I know somet'ing about women—not to brag."

"If you are so anxious to see dat young lady, Felix," said another, "you don't need to walk so far. She is, at dis moment, wid her father an' her stepmudder, on dis trip."

"What! what you say? Well, wait. I di'n' inten', me, to dress for de ladies' cabin to-night, mais when I have my supper I will put on my Sunday t'ings—jus' to go an' sit down in de cabin w'ere—I—can—look—at innocent—beauty! It pleasure me, yas, to see some t'ing like dat. Maybe I am not all good, mais I am not all given over for bad so long I can enjoy a rose-vine all in pink, or a fair yo'ng girl more beautiful yet.

"I tell you, my friends, I was sitting, week before las', at my 'ouse on Esplanade Street, on de back gallerie, w'ere de vines is t'ick, an' dey were, as you might say, honey-suckling de bees—an' de perfume from my night-bloomin' jasmine filled my nose. It was in de evening, an' de moon on de blue sky was like a map of de city, jus' a silver crescent, an' close by, one li'l' star, shining, as de children say, 'like a diamond in de sky,' an' I tell you—I tell you—

"Well, I tell you, I wished I had been a good man all my life!"

His friends laughed gaily at this.

"You don' say!" laughed one. "Well, you fooled us, any'ow! I was holding my breat'. I t'ought somet'ing was getting ready to happen!"

"Well—an' ain't dat somet'ing?—when a hard ol' sinner like me can see in nature a t'ing sweet an' good an'—an' resolute himself!"

"Sure, dat is a great happening; mais for such a beginning, so dramatic, we expected to see Hamlet—or maybe his father's ghost—or somet'ing!"

"I am thinking more of this exceptional beauty"—it was the American who interrupted now—"I am more interested in her than in the confessions of old sinners like ourselves. I am rather practical, and beauty is only skin-deep—sometimes at least. I should like to take a peep at this rare product of our State. Louisiana's record up to date is hard to beat, in this respect."

"Well," slowly remarked the man known throughout as Felix, "I am not telling! If I knew, I could not tell, and, of co'se, it is all guess-work, mais you may believe me or not—" he lowered his voice, suggesting mystery. "I say you can riffuse to believe me or not, I was—well, I was not long ago, one day, sitting at de table down at Leon's,—eating an oyster wid a friend of mine, and, looking out of de window, I happened to see, sitting in a tree, one li'l' bird—jus' one small li'l' bird, no bigger dan yo' t'umb.

"I was not t'inking about de bird, mind you. We were jus' talking about anyt'ing in partic'lar—I mean to say nothing in general. What is de matter wid me to-day? I cannot talk straight—my tongue is all twis'. I say we were speaking of partic'lar t'ings in general, an' he remarked to me, 'Who you t'ink will be de Queen of de Carnival dis coming Mardi Gras?'

"I was pouring a glass of Château Yquem at de time,—to look after de oysters,—an' I di'n' pay so much attention to what he was saying—I can never pour a glass an' speak at de same time. I spill my words or de wine, sure. So it happened dat when I put me de bottle down, my eye passed out de window. Oh, hush! No, not my eye, of co'se—I mean my sight. Well, dat li'l' bird it was still waiting in the same place, in de magnolia-tree, an' when I looked, it give me one glance, sideways, like a finger on de nose, an' it opened wide its bill, an' just so plain as I am speaking now, it spoke a name." This in still lower voice.

"But I said nothing, immediately. A little wine, for a few glasses, it make me prudent—up to a certain point, of co'se. Mais, direc'ly, I looked at my friend, an' wid what you might call an air of nonchalance, I repeat to him de name exac'ly as it was tol' to me by de li'l' bird in de magnolia-tree. An' wa't you t'ink he said?"

"Oh, go on. What he say?"

"You want to know what he said? Well, dat I can tell you. He was greatly astonish', an' he whispered to me, 'Who tol' you? You are not in de Pickwick?'"

"Oh, a little bird tol' me!" I answered him. "No, I am not in de club."

"But the name? Do tell us!"

"Oh, no. I cannot. If I told, dat would be telling, eh?"

"Sure! It is not necessary," said another. "Well, I am pleased, me."

"An' me!"

"I like always to listen when you tell somet'ing, Felix. Your story is all right—an' I believe you. I always believe any man in de Pickwick Club—on some subjects! Mais, ol' man, de nex' time you make a story at Leon's restaurant, suppose you move off dat magnolia-tree. A bird could stand on de window-sill across de street jus' as well—a real window-sill."

"T'ank you. I am sure a real somet'ing-to-stand-on would be better for a real bird. Mais, for dis particular bird, I t'ink my magnolia is more suitable. Don't forget de story of de Mongoose!"

"Nobody can get ahead of you, Felix. Well, it is a good t'ing. It is true, her fodder was de King at las' year's Carnival—an' it is lightning striking twice in de same place; an' yet—"

"And yet," the American interrupted, "and yet it will sometimes strike twice in the same place—if the attraction is sufficient. I have a friend who has a summer home in the Tennessee mountains which was twice struck—three times, nearly. That is the house next door got it the third time. And then they began to investigate, and they found the mountain full of iron—iron convertible into gold."

"Well, and our man of iron, let us hope he may prove always an attraction—for bolts of good fortune!"

"A wish that may come true; if reports be correct, he is rapidly turning into gold," said the American. "I am told that he has found salt in immense deposits on his island—and that he has resumed the work begun just before the war— that of opening up the place."

"Oh, yas. 'Tis true. Over a hundred t'ousand dollars he has already put in—an' as much more ready to drop. Mais it is fairyland! An' me, I was t'inking too— sometimes I t'ink a little myself—I was t'inking dat if—I say if sometime his daughter would be de Comus Queen, not insinuating anything, you know—no allusion to de bird—what a fine house-party dey could have now, eh? Dey could invite de royal party, maids of honor, and so fort'—whoever is rich enough to lose so much time—

"T'ink of sailing up de new canal on de barge—"

"An' under de bridge—"

"No, not de bridge. He will never touch dat. He has made a new plan, entering another way. Dat span of de bridge he commenced—it is standing beside de beautiful w'ite marble tomb—to hold his family. His wife she is dere, an' de ol' negroes what care for his chil'—dey are laying in one corner, wid also a small monument."

"Are you sure dey are dere?"

"I have seen de monument, I tell you."

"Well, Harold he was always sentimental, if you will. I suppose dat broken bridge is, as he says—it is history, and he needs to keep it before him, not to be too rash. Maybe so. Who can tell? Two boys in de war, it was enough—if he had stopped to t'ink."

"Yas—mais de barge, de Cleopatra; dey say she is be'-u-tiful!"

"Cleopatra! For what he di'n' name her somet'ing sensible?"

"Dat is not only sensible—it is diplomatic. You know, when a man has only a daughter and a step-wife—what is de matter wid me to-night? You understand me. I say, in—well, in some cases, to discriminate, it is enough to drive a man to—"

"Oh, don't say dat, Felix."

"Let me finish, will you? I say it is one of dose indelicate situations dat drive a man to dodge! An' when he can dodge into history and romance at once, so much de better! An' Cleopatra, it sound well for a barge. An' so, really, if de beautiful daughter should be de queen an' dey could arrange one house-party—"

"Suppose, Felix, ol' man, you would bring out yo' magnolia-tree once more, you don't t'ink de li'l' bird would come again an' stan' on one limb an' maybe—"

"Ah, no. I am sure not. If dey had a grain of salt in dat story, I would try. I would put it on his tail. Mais, how can you catch a bird widout salt?"

76

So idly, playfully, the talk rippled on, ever insensibly flavored with rich romance of life, even as the fitful breeze skirting the shores held, in shy suspension, an occasional hint of orange-blossoms or of the Cuban fruits which, heaping the luggers in the slanting sun, laid their gay bouquets of color against the river's breast.

It is many years since the maid Agnes Le Duc, on her way to coronation at the carnival, stood while the sun went down in all her vestal beauty on deck of the Laurel Hill, and smiled through tears of tenderness at life as half revealed to her.

Many things are changed since then, and yet the great river flows on, all unheeding.

Laden to their guards, so that their weighty cargoes of cotton and sugar, traveling to mill and to market, are wet with the spray of playful condescension, panting ships of commerce, some flying foreign colors, still salute each other in passing, with ever a word of solicitude as to milady's health.

Old Lady Mississippi, is she high or low in spirits? And will her hand of benediction turn to smite and to despoil?

But, whether she be obdurate or kindly, hysterical or melancholy, or so serene as to invite the heavens, life and love and song are hers.

Uniting while she seems to divide, bringing together whom she appears to separate, a raft of logs contributed by her grace affording free passage the length of her realm to whoever will take it, paying no toll, she invites Romance to set sail under the stars in primal simplicity, eschewing the "bridal chambers" of white and gold which lie in the hearts of all the busy steamers, no matter how otherwise prosaic their personalities.

And still, afloat and alongshore, astride a molasses-barrel or throwing dice between the cotton-bales, taking no thought of the morrow, the negro sings:

"Cometh our fount of every blessing!"

Milton Keynes UK
Ingram Content Group UK Ltd.
UKHW010702260923
429409UK00004B/388